# Elephants in Our Bedroom

# Elephants in Our Bedroom

stories by

# Michael Czyzniejewski

DZANC
BOOKS

DZANC
BOOKS
1334 Woodbourne Street
Westland, MI 48186
www.dzancbooks.org

Some of the stories in this collection have appeared, perhaps in a slightly different form, in the following publications: /nor, Issue 2, Fall 2007: "Wind," *Alaska Quarterly Review*, Volume 26, Numbers 1 & 2, Spring/Summer 2009: "Nectarine Pie," *American Literary Review*, Volume XVI, Issue 2, Fall 2005: "Green," *American Short Fiction*, Issue 37, Spring 2007: "The Death of Purple," *Another Chicago Magazine*, No. 40, Spring 2002: "Dave Corzine Does Not Live Here," *Bat City Review*, Issue 2, Spring 2006: "pleurisy," *The Bellingham Review*, Volume XXXII, Issue 61, Spring 2009: "Cwm," *The Greensboro Review*, Number 80, Fall 2006: "Cool," *Lake Effect*, Volume 13, Spring 2009: "Hapax Legomenon," MississippiReview.com, Volume 11, Number 2, Spring 2005: "Finding My Werewolf Mask in the Hide-a-Bed, July 4, 1994," *Monkeybicycle*, Issue 6, Winter 2008: "Valentine," *New Orleans Review*, Volume 31, Number 1, Summer 2005: "Fight," *New South*, Volume 1, Number 1, Fall/Winter 2007: "The Magic of Oil Painting," *Northwest Review*, Volume 24, Number 3, Fall 2004: "B positive," *Other Voices*, Volume 20, Number 46, Spring/Summer 2007: "My Lover's Name," *Post Road*, Issue Number 15, Spring/Summer 2008: "Victor," *Quick Fiction*, Issue 9, Spring 2006: "Prison Romance" and Issue 11, Spring 2007: "Sleeping Through Starvation," *The Southern Review*, Volume 44:4—Fall 2008: "The Elephant in Our Bedroom," *StoryQuarterly*, Number 35, 1998: "Streetfishing," *Western Humanities Review*, Volume LIX, Number 2, Fall 2005: "In My Lover's Bedroom," "Fight" was reprinted in *The Pushcart Prize XXXI: Best of the Small Presses.*

First edition February 2009 by Dzanc Books
Book design by Steven Seighman
Cover painting by Nancy Wartman: "Elephants in Our Bedroom"
Watercolor/Colored Pencil 22" x 29" 2008
06 07 08 09 10 11 5 4 3 2 1
ISBN: 0-9793123-7-x
ISBN-13: 978-0-9793123-7-3
Printed in the United States of America

# Table of Contents

Wind *9*

Streetfishing *13*

Valentine *20*

Sleepmurder *25*

The Elephant in Our Bedroom *42*

B positive *45*

Dave Corzine Does Not Live Here *62*

Green *76*

The Summer Without Grown-Ups *79*

Victor *103*

Cool *117*

In My Lover's Bedroom *121*

Prison Romance *125*

The Magic of Oil Painting *127*

My Lover's Name *131*

Nectarine Pie *136*

Finding My Werewolf Mask in the Hide-a-Bed, July 4, 1994 *145*

Cwm *153*

Sleeping Through Starvation *158*

pleurisy *160*

Fight *165*

Hapax Legomenon *167*

What Haunts Me in New Hampshire *190*

The Death of Purple *199*

For Smitty.
Wish you could have been here.

# Wind

All of a sudden, nobody can explain wind. For better or worse, we've experienced wind, for years. Centuries, really. Always. The whole time, we just assumed someone knew where it came from, that scientists, the meteorologists probably, maybe even DaVinci, someone had written it down somewhere. *Wind is a type of weather caused by* _____. Not so. There's nothing— no encyclopedia entries, no conjecture, not even attempts to explain it. Other weather, we have the data, the answer to the question. How hot or cold it is mostly depends on how close we are to the sun, while rain is a build-up of moisture in the air. Snow, well, that's just cold rain. Wind, though, we never knew. Ever.

I'm watching the special news report, the kind they break into television shows for, like for when a president dies, when I hear the thud: My infant son has rolled over and fallen off the couch. This is new—no rolling over before, just stationary baby slumber. The thud sounds like a bowling ball slamming against a wet lawn, and before I can even turn my head from the TV, my boy is screaming, an impossible scream from something so small and lying with his face flat down. I scramble and lift him to my chest, thinking at the same time I shouldn't move him, that if he's broken, I'll only make it worse, spread the fracture, disperse the hemorrhage. But I can't just leave him on the ground to scream, helpless. He's alone, needing his daddy, plus: the neighbors could hear. In my arms, his skin is hot and red and he is oblivious to me, to my shushes, my hand wrapped around his head, pushing his face into my face, his tears rolling in my mouth. I dance with my son, sway and pace, hoping he is more stunned than injured, the thud the worst part for us both. Babies are supposed to bounce, the story goes; because they're so fragile, so defenseless, they can withstand trauma that adults, even older kids, never could. I hope this is true, not some wives' tale, and I haven't killed my son the first time he and I are alone together.

When I was eleven, my own father shot himself in his office. He was mayor of our town, a five-termer, the son of the previous mayor, himself the son of the village founder and postmaster. My father was sixty-eight when I was eleven, my mother his second wife, only thirty, the first wife dead from lupus and their children grown and long gone. Like most towns, we had debt, we had crime, and one town over always seemed like a better place to live. But my father was honest and did what he could to keep the roads paved, taxes low, bright lights on the downtown trees in December. No one had been murdered in our town in my lifetime, and as far as anyone knew, no industry was pouring chemicals into the groundwater. He was going to run again the next year, for a sixth term, like his father, and he would have won, though it's doubtful anyone would have challenged.

The morning my father shot himself, he sat down to breakfast like he always did, one eye on the paper and the other on me, and asked what I planned on accomplishing that day. I remember telling him I would ace my science test, resist trading my ham sandwich for a dessert, and, when I came home, do my homework before I even thought about turning on the idiot box. My father told me it was a good plan, one he'd sign off on, push before the city council with zest and zeal. An hour later he was dead. They pulled me out of school as soon as they heard, interrupted my science test, the principal breaking the news in the hall then driving me home in her baby blue Chevette. A policewoman and a psychologist were waiting for me, and we sat in the kitchen making small talk for almost five hours until my mom came home. They didn't know where to find her, didn't have a daytime number. She didn't know about my dad until she found us all at the table, the window open, finishing off the strawberry pie from the ledge. To this day, I don't know where my mom was in that time, gone for five hours when I'd always assumed she was waiting for me, cooking, cleaning, talking to other city officials' wives on the phone. She's still alive—I could ask her if I wanted to, and she'd probably tell me. But it's something I didn't want to know, so I never asked, and I don't think I ever will.

   I am not the mayor of my town. Neither are any of my stepbrothers, all of whom I've met exactly once, at my father's funeral years ago. I am not fit to be mayor, let alone the father of a three-month-old, a tiny cluster of skin and eyes and sharp, sharp fingernails, and like his father, not very much hair, though he's moving in the opposite direction. Ten minutes after my son slams into the carpet, he stops screaming. He goes from frenzy to all-out laughing just as quickly as he's discovered rolling over. I search for signs of concussion, or at least what I think are signs of concussion, bloodshot eyes, vomiting, a loss of balance, which, I decide, would be impossible to determine. In all respects, my son appears fine, cheery and adoring, his only souvenir a heart-shaped abrasion on his forehead, a small patch of red, more of a carpet burn, I settle on, than a sign of internal bleeding.

   Later, when my wife comes home and sees the heart, she pulls him from my arms, grasping him as tightly as I had, demanding to know what I'd done. Had I not let my son roll off the couch and hit his head on the floor, I would have demanded to know why she was gone for two hours instead of a half, what her plan was in case something went wrong, our only car gone with her, the family phone in her purse. But the heart is something I must explain, her absence a secondary concern, secondary at best. I first try to pretend that it doesn't exist, that the heart's an impression of my chin on his forehead, or maybe a rash, a reaction to the new, off-brand detergent. My wife does not believe me. When she presses, demands to know what I did to our son, I tell her the only thing that makes any sense to me, the only thing that she will accept, sooner or later. I tell her *I don't know*, that it's something we may never, ever find out.

# Streetfishing

It was Friday night, so me and Trap were streetfishing out in front of my house. Trap'd just cast his line into the old wicker laundry basket that served as our target, his ocean hook (which I thought was cheating) and fifty-pound test grabbing onto one of the handles, dragging it along Oasis Street like a 30-inch bass. It was Trap's fourth catch of the night, putting me four behind, but since there was plenty of beer in our cooler and our wives had left, possibly for good, I had nothing but time to catch up.

Trap reeled the basket down the street, mocking me. "It's not official until you get it in the boat," he said. I laughed along, waiting for my turn, a Zebco 4000 in one hand, an Old Style in the other, planning the comeback that would take us into the later hours of the warm, breezy evening.

That's when these women showed up, in their souped-up station wagon, speeding around the corner from behind us, nearly knocking me and Trap into the next work week. The driver tapped her brakes, giving us slim opportunity to dive onto opposite lawns, me in front of my house, Trap on Warren's, the old neighbor who sits in his window and watches our world from the other side of the street. As we hit the ground, the wagon tore past, crushing an array of beer bottles, accelerating into the old wicker basket—still hooked to Trap's rod and reel—sending it high into the air, wicker shards flying like Pixie Sticks. Trap held tight to his rod, the station wagon dragging his scrawny frame across the grass, slamming his head into the iron post under Warren's mailbox. The pole remained in his fist, snapping the fifty-pound test, slingshotting the basket, what was left of it, into the black sky, arcing it off into the retention pond where me and Trap would cast when there was water being retented.

"Son of a bitch," Trap said, jumping up, still clenching his rod, his free hand on top of his head. Even from where I was lying, I could see blood gleaming off his palm in the light from the corner lamppost.

I stumbled back to the street to spy where the women were headed. Their brake lights got smaller and smaller as they sped down Oasis, out of our lives, which gave us no chance for vengeance. Drunk blondies out on a bender, no care in the world.

Trap dragged himself like Igor and joined me in the street.

"You'll need stronger test if you want to land that mother," I told him.

"Go to hell, Fergis," Trap said and brought his hand down, holding it in front of us. Blood coated it like a rubber glove, dripping down his wrist, and from his head, into his eyes. "Did you get a look at them?"

"They were women," I said. "In the station wagon from hell."

Trap dropped his rod and reel onto the ground—something I'd never seen him do—and placed his hand on top of his head, smearing blood over his cheek with the other. "Did you catch anything useful? A license plate?"

"I saw what you saw," I said.

Trap nodded and slashed his arm across his bloody temple once more. He bent to pick up his rod, but when he stood upright, his knees wobbled and shook, timbering him into me, the blood smearing my white tank.

"Are you OK?" I asked.

"I'm still here, ain't I?"

"I mean, are we done for the evening?" Four hits behind, I wanted a chance to redeem myself.

"We've never let women speeding away in a car ruin a night before, have we, Fergis?"

Trap's head was still bleeding like beer from a tap.

"Start from scratch?" I said.

"Four-zip, cheater. Your cast."

"What's the new target?"

"That sewer cap," Trap said, pointing. "If you graze it on the way back, it counts."

I got another Style from the Lil Oscar on the curb. Then I cast. My tackle plopped down three feet to the right of the sewer and five feet past.

"Bulrushes," Trap said. "If we were on Powderhorn, you'd've lost that lure in the weeds."

I reeled my line in, sipping beer, ignoring Trap. My hook and sinker sped along the pavement, skipping into the glass, blood, and other debris. About fifteen feet in front of us, my line stopped, pulled tight, and changed direction, sailing back away from us.

"I think you got something," Trap said. He leaned forward and squinted his bloodied eyes.

Something *was* grabbing onto my line, in the middle of Oasis Street, weaving the tip of my pole. I pulled back on my rod and forced something out of the street, into the air.

"You got a bluegill," Trap said, placing his beer down, glancing around, as if for a net.

Trap was right. I had a bluegill on the end of my hook, struggling, jumping, having made that crucial mistake.

"I'll be damned," I said. I reeled it all the way in and dangled the fish in front of me, spinning it around on my line in mini-figure eights.

"A keeper," Trap said. "Near nine inches."

"I'll stick him in the cooler," I said, then did so, taking out the last two Styles. "Your cast."

Trap's reel launched, tackle flying far into the sky, landing on the other end of the block. He clicked the button and waited, staring out into Oasis' dark stretches. I drank my beer and thought I'd finally outdone my friend. Trap's line slacked, spirals coiling looser and looser. His bobber drifted, ignored.

"I'd better get this in," he said.

On its way back, right in the middle of the blood and broken glass, something snagged Trap's line, spinning and whirring his reel, Trap caught unaware.

"Hold my legs," Trap yelled, jerked forward by whatever had his line. He reclicked and pulled back on the rod with all his leverage. The tip of the pole gave, arching, quivering, ready to snap, Trap alternating between turns of his reel and more pulls. I gripped his legs, keeping him out of the water.

Fifteen minutes and a whole lot of fifty-pound test later, Trap pulled something the size of a barracuda out of the street, the fish as long as one of my legs, its fin ready to cut a man in half. A marlin, I was sure.

"The net, Fergis," Trap ordered, the catch as heavy as he was.

"Drop him in the cooler," I said and let Trap go, reaching for the Lil Oscar. I removed the lid and dragged it under the marlin. Trap lowered the tail into the ice, pulled his knife off his belt, and cut the fifty-pound test. The marlin slid into the ice at the bottom, pushing aside my gill.

Before Trap could even start retelling the story, I cast my line out into the broken glass.

"I've never caught a fish that big," Trap said, then after a few seconds, added, "at least not that you've seen."

But I wasn't listening, another bite biting, my bobberless line bending down to the ground, its tip shaking like a divining rod. I pulled in some slack, then jerked back and cranked in another bluegill, this one bigger than the last by four inches, its belly bright like fresh-squeezed orange juice.

"Take a look at this," I said and held up the gill, more like fifteen inches now that I had him close.

Trap wasn't watching. He'd gone back inside for his tackle and was refixing his line, tying on a hook as big as my pointer and thumb, a roll of seventy-pound test off to the side.

"You're using the wrong type of pole, Fergis. You're getting stuff for the pan. I'm pulling in things for the wall."

I looked down at my gill, the biggest I'd ever caught, picturing the fillets I'd get with a few dozen like him. My dad had raised me on lakes. The thought of casting with one of Trap's ocean rods made me sick. "You fish how you want to," I said. "I'll do the same."

"Suit yourself." Trap reclicked his reel and released his line and monster hook into the glassy bloodwater. Not even giving him a chance to solidify his footing, something pulled the line down the hole, again almost taking Trap with it. I dropped my gill into the cooler and took hold of Trap's net, waiting for him to pull out another lunker. This time he'd nailed a sailfish, as long as the marlin, maybe not as thick. Trap knifed him into the cooler, my newly-bobbered line already out and under.

This is the way it went for several hours. I pulled out lakefish—bluegill, cat, walleye, muskie, mackerel, pike, perch, plus the occasional carp, tossing those under my pine for the raccoons, not wanting that garbage polluting my new spot. Trap had his sights set higher, slaying more marlin and sailfish, as well as cusk, snook, tuna, grouper, red snapper, Alaskan pollack, some we couldn't name, and one five-foot hammerhead shark, too dangerous to be in the Lil Oscar. Trap gutted that bastard with his knife and slashed his line, returning it to the drink. The cooler filled quickly without it, but there was still plenty room for more.

We should have tired out, especially after Trap hit the killer whale, almost the end of both of us, but a good spot is a good spot, and we weren't going to leave until the fish did.

By nine a.m., cars started pulling onto Oasis, using our street as they always did, to get somewhere else, except waving and turning around now, off in search of new routes. A couple guys pulled over to watch, some with poles and tackle boxes at the ready. We made it clear, however, the street—through some made-up Gaming Division loophole—was our private property. They were welcome to stick around and spectate, maybe even put in an order: The Lil Oscar was bursting with enough to fill our freezers and our dens. The reporters and photographers took to this idea more than anyone, flashing a roll of film every time we landed another prize, asking our names, ages, what we did for a living. We enjoyed the attention, but not as much as the sport. Best fishing we'd ever had.

When old Warren came out, an ice pole in one hand, a mesh salmon basket in the other, we couldn't tell him no. It was his street, too, plenty of fish for the three of us. Me and Trap took five to shoot a spot for the TV people, and we watched to see how the old man would fare. I hoped he'd get some salmon, enough even to swap for a few of my gill.

"You're an old fool," Martha, his wife of fifty-five years, called out their window. "You have me inside, and you're out fishing in the middle of the street."

Warren fished on, but what she said seemed to take some effect. No matter how long he waited or how many times he dropped, his bobber sat stationary on the cement, rolling in the occasional breeze, as if on a solid surface.

"Quiet, woman," Warren called back. "You're scaring the fish away."

Trap cast back in after about ten minutes of this, impatient as Warren's wife, crowding my old neighbor with longer range and a bigger hook. Warren reeled in his line, shook his head and headed home, swearing under his breath. I wished him a good morning, then watched as his wife held the door open and let it hit him in the ass on his way in.

Trap wasn't getting a bite.

His hook and sinker lingered on the cement like Warren's bobber, the water hard, a wall. I held fast with my pole, watching Trap not get as much as a nibble from a guppy.

"What do you think?" Trap said, rolling his neck in its socket. He swished his hook with frenzied pulls.

I wanted to cast, but was afraid. "I think we've been out here a long time," I said, watching Trap's hook. A few of the fans returned to their cars. Warren's drapes, always slit open, closed. "Maybe we need to move?"

Trap pulled on his hook, then reeled in and recast. Still nothing. "I'm getting tired, Fergis. Maybe now's a good time for a break."

"Maybe," I said, looking at how much blood covered Trap, his clothes, the street. I wondered how he was even standing.

I hooked my hook onto an eyehole, handing the pole to Trap to take inside. I said, "I'll get the cooler."

Trap took my pole, looking at the cooler, then up at me. I walked over and bent at my knees, knowing how heavy it would be with my bad back, then glanced over my shoulder at Trap.

"Go ahead, Fergis. Pick it up."

I faked a smile, then turned back to the cooler. I pushed my hands onto the handles, hesitating to lift, hoping I'd need Trap's help, that it would be heavier than anything I could lift by myself, not wanting to go it alone.

# Valentine

For the third year in a row, my wife visits her gynecologist on Valentine's Day. Not that I'm keeping track, but since we've known each other just over three years, it's been hard not to notice. The first year, when we were still dating, it seemed like a fluke, scheduling without thinking, perhaps without caring. The next year, I thought it a strange coincidence, but Valerie thinks it's much stranger that I remember the date of her female appointments. True, but I did some investigating and found out that for healthy women, the gynecologist is a once-a-year visit. It all made sense: Valerie schedules her yearly appointment on the way out, just says, *Same time, next year*, and her date just so happens to be February 14th. So by the third year, I'm not surprised. In fact, on the night of the 13th, I ask Valerie what time her appointment is the next day. She asks how I know about her appointment and I lie and say she'd mentioned it to me that morning. She doesn't believe me, but I convince her. *How else would I know?* I say. My wife goes to bed suspicious, but my prediction is confirmed: Valentine's Day is her day to see her OB-GYN. I'm OK with that, I decide, because there's nothing not to be OK about.

Only, the OB-GYN, from what I've been told, from what I've seen in movies and on TV, never makes for a pleasant experience. Not that any doctor's visit ever does. But this type of doctor involves lying in a paper robe on a table, lifting your legs into stirrups, and letting a doctor—I'm not sure if Valerie's is a man or a woman—put things—fingers and instruments—up inside you. If nothing's wrong, it's the worst experience you'll have all week. If an irregularity is detected, the whole adventure goes downhill quickly. The thought of my wife going through that, mere hours before we turn up the romance dial, makes me pause. And that's all.

My wife and I are young and haven't been married long, so we don't wait for birthdays, anniversaries, or Valentine's Day to have sex. But we *do* do it on those days. Valerie doesn't seem affected by her doctor's visits—she performs with the same vigor, the same tenderness and love, never straying too much from what we've agreed upon, what we've both come to expect. Close observation on those days has produced no noticeable variation. If anything, Valentine's Day sex with Valerie is only slightly better than sex with her on any other day. Maybe it's because Valentine's Day brings out something special, the romance in the air, that extra fuel. Maybe it's the roses and box of chocolates. But maybe—and I know I shouldn't think this— maybe it's the gynecologist. It could be she's had an occasion to think about her body all day, or perhaps she has a thing for her gynie, and each Valentine's Night, she's thinking of him (or her) when we embrace. I don't know. But since there's really no way to tell, it's a subject better forgotten.

Two days later, I take a personal day and drop by Valerie's OB-GYN. Knowing myself as I do, it's a miracle I waited till the 16th. When I get to the office, I'm shocked. The vision I'd been toting around couldn't be more false. Instead of the dim lighting, burgundy wallpaper, and smooth jazz I'd expected for the waiting room, I find a more staid atmosphere, one you'd find at a podiatrist or chiropractor. Valerie's doctor has not decorated since the late '80s, I deduce, from the teal and fuchsia wallpaper, the plastic ferns and faded Nagel prints. I also imagined a whole slew of women, varied in age and appearance, all of them nervous to get inside, their one-year wait at its long, long end. No harem awaits, however, just one woman and her teenage daughter. When I step inside, the mother/daughter stare at me with unhidden distrust, pinching their legs together and taking account of their personal belongings. I think about saying something like, *Oops! Wrong office!* or pretending to be some sort of delivery man, but that's not going to help me sleep later that night, or allow me to make love to Valerie the next time with a clear conscience.

My only outlet, I decide, is to ask to see the doctor. Given that most women, like my wife, make these appointments a year ahead of time, it's doubtful the receptionist is used to walk-ups. I suppose women come down with sudden issues, yeast infections and missed periods and other things I don't want to think about. But from a guy? I can't blame her for the furled brow.

The receptionist, about thirty years past retirement, asks how she can help me. I tell her I want to see the doctor and she giggles, pointing out that I am at a gynecologist's. When I tell her I know, that I *need* to see the doctor, she immediately pecks two numbers on her phone, whispers something into the receiver, then slides shut the glass divider between her and me. She asks through the notches why I want to see the doctor, and because I have nothing else to say, I tell her it's an emergency. She rolls three or four feet backward, making sure her skirt hasn't run up on her, exposing too much leg. The mother and her daughter inch toward the door, and when I turn and look at them, they freeze. I open my mouth to say something, and one of them sits back down while the other, the daughter, makes a beeline for the hallway. On her way out, she avoids collision with a security guard, who does not pinch his legs, does not envelope his belongings. Taking one last shot in the dark, I say to the guard, *It's an emergency, I swear*, which, in retrospect, probably made the situation worse instead of better.

When I was a kid, my mother let me believe in Santa Claus until I was thirteen. Since I was home-schooled and didn't partake in many out-of-school activities—no Little League, no Cub Scouts, no karate—nobody made me any the wiser. I had to be the only kid in my town, if not my state, who had pubic hair, popped zits in the mirror, and masturbated two or three times a day, all the while still thinking Santa was the one delivering those toys and games and knitted sweaters. My mom had to show me the receipts from the stores before I believed her. Later, in college, I went in truly believing that I was going to be a doctor, that I was going to help sick people and make a lot of money doing it. Even senior year, my GPA stuck somewhere around 2.0, I kept telling everyone, especially myself, I was going to get into med school. Someday I was going to have a license to cut people open with a knife and repair their hearts. For money. My parents are in their fifties now and I'm convinced they are going to live forever, despite the fact my dad has ALS and probably won't last the year. I grew up a Cubs fan.

My overall optimism, blind and stupid, sometimes overpowers my craziness. It's what makes it possible for me to leave the gynecologist's, head home, and propose lovemaking to Valerie. Not lovemaking, actually, but sex. Like I said, we weren't married long enough to wait for holidays, but twice in three days is pushing it for not being on vacation. I don't wait until after dinner and TV, either. I walk in the door, throw my jacket on the floor, and ask Valerie, straight out, if she wants to do it and do it now. I make a motion to the bedroom with my head and loosen my tie.

To my surprise, Valerie doesn't laugh. Instead, she puts down her magazine, takes a gulp out of a mixed drink on the coffee table, and lifts off her blouse. She doesn't stop to go to the bathroom, nor does she fix herself in the mirror. She hurries to our bedroom, finishes disrobing, and curls onto the bed, smiling and patting the empty space next to her. Not since our honeymoon has sex with Valerie been so unnegotiated.

Valerie's performance holds steady. Perhaps a notch lower than the night before the last, but nothing I'd complain about. I revisit my Valentine's Day theory, the romance and the chocolate, and decide maybe it's all been in my head. After, even though I'm wiped, it's too early to go to sleep. We lie on the blankets, next to one another, and Valerie says, *That was a pleasant surprise.* This is the first critique, positive or negative, she has ever offered, though later, I'll wonder if she's referring to my performance being surprising, or the impulse in general.

Her head on my shoulder, Valerie tells me about work, how one of the other teachers is getting a divorce, how a fifth grader got caught with a *Hustler* in his locker. I think about my day the whole time she talks, but when she asks about it, I don't bring up my adventure. I do not tell her about the personal day, my run-in with security, or how her gynecologist, looking less like Fabio than any man alive, appeared in the waiting room and kept me from being escorted out. How he took me back to one of the examination rooms, sat me on the cold, metal table, and asked me what kind of emergency I had that he could help me with. We talked for ten minutes, about this and that, and I think I learned a lot. Instead of sharing that info, I tell my wife that I believed in Santa until I was thirteen, and when she says I'm lying, I tell her I swear. When she still doesn't buy it, I reach to my pants for my phone and punch my mother's number, one on speed dial. When Mom picks up and says hello, I hand the phone to Valerie, who grunts out, *Wrong number* and clicks END. *Don't be crazy*, she says and swears that she believes me. I don't believe that she believes me, but I let it go, wondering, as Valerie gets up and peels into her underwear, if there's any way I'll ever be able to find out for sure.

# Sleepmurder

**M**y husband is a sleepwalker, and every night since we've been married, he has attempted to murder me in our bed. Exactly two hours after he falls asleep, Erik sits up, takes hold of his pillow, and stuffs it into my face. So far, he's never pushed hard enough or long enough to succeed, but when you've been through what I've been through, you might at least consider it's the thought that counts. After thirty seconds, the pillow always disappears, and Erik always falls back to sleep, waking for work at 6:50, all smiles, pecks, and pep. Needless to say, Erik hasn't ever killed me, and I'm confident he never will. The pillow routine is just a part of my life, one I accept, like getting my period or being 4'11". I'd change them all if I could, but in the end, I can't.

Two common misconceptions about sleepwalking exist. The first is that the sleepwalker performs actual walking, traveling from their place of sleep to another location. This is false. Sixteen percent of humans sleepwalk, but most of them commit more simple acts, either sitting up in bed or just raising their arms into the air, ceasing this behavior within seconds.

Since nobody considers this sleepwalking, these cases are hardly ever reported. While some sleepwalkers perform elaborate tasks such as doing the dishes or even driving, most of the other stuff comes off as mundane, more sleepgesturing than anything else.

The second misconception is that a sleepwalker should never be awakened. Rumor has it, the walker will react violently, hurting or perhaps killing the waker. In truth, not a single doctor in the vast history of sleep study has ever produced a case where a woken walker has ever harmed anyone. Disoriented, yes. Embarrassed, yes. But violent, no. While Erik would be devastated to know what he's doing, his pride would be the only thing hurt if I ever decided to wake him. So I don't.

Before our wedding day, Erik thought I was a virgin. One hundred percent, I went with the whole I'm-saving-myself-for-marriage bit. Whenever someone talked about sex, in real life or on TV, I acted uncomfortable, turning my head, grimacing, changing the subject (or channel), writing off such a topic as low class. In fact, I'd had a lot of boyfriends—in high school, in college, the few years since, and trust me, all of them—save the one from Bible camp in ninth grade—got what they were brave enough to take. A first-year psychology student could tell you that I lied to Erik because I wanted him to respect me, wanted a fresh start with the man I was going to marry. But it's not that simple. I admit, Erik wouldn't have married me if he knew about the forty-seven men I'd slept with before our meeting. But really, it's more about the control. I just wanted to know something that Erik didn't. Once he heard I was a virgin and wanted to stay that way until our wedding night, he bought into it. He changed the way he talked, the way he dressed, the way he carried himself in general. He started buying me things: flowers, bracelets, dinner. He opened the door for me, held my hand in public. He stopped swearing, if "damn" and "hell" are swear words. He even bought a book on tape that we listened to when we drove to his parents' in Ohio, a book about abstinence written for Mennonite teenagers. And just so things would be as special for him as they would be for me, he promised not to masturbate—and I believe he kept this promise—not having a waking orgasm for three-and-half-months before our big day. For a guy, that's murder, over a hundred days. More than I love him, I loved the fact that he did all this, that he jumped through all these hoops, for me.

But I also love that I was willing to make him do it, and had the self-control to see it through. I've never stuck with a plan in my life, from exercise routines, to quitting smoking, to a major in college—I changed mine six times and still settled on communications. But for close to a year, I convinced my fiancé I'd never had sex. Cruel, yes, but a milestone in my personal development. And all this before he ever tried to murder me in his sleep.

The first time Erik tried to sleepmurder me, it was our wedding night. Our reception raging on without us, we were at the Hilton by the airport, our flight to Jamaica at 6:30 the next morning. To be honest, when the pillow came down, sleepwalking never entered my mind—I just assumed Erik was trying to kill me. Maybe he found out about the other guys or he just realized I was lying to him. Or maybe he was just nuts. It happens, why not to me?

Before the pillow hit my face, I was awake for an instant, long enough to know what was happening. I thought about kicking, but within an instant, I accepted my fate: Erik was too good to be true, and this is what I got for believing I deserved him. Girls like me never meet Mom and Dad, let alone move in and share a checking account. Somewhere, there was an insurance policy. That had to be it.

When the pillow came off my face, I rolled to the floor and ran to the other side of our room, grabbing my cell from the nightstand, along with the best weapon I could find: the room service menu in a leather ledger. Hyperventilating, I couldn't dial a nine, a one, and a one in sequence, messing up five times, all the while slashing the ledger into the air like Zorro. After ten minutes, when I heard Erik snoring, I stopped trying to reach the police. At first I thought it was a ruse, him hoping I'd call off calling the cops. But it kept up. After ten minutes, the snore had me convinced. That's when I started to put things together. To be sure, I curled into a fetal position under the desk, staring at my new husband the whole time, looking for signs of movement, of faking. I managed to fall asleep when the sun came up, convincing myself he wouldn't try it again during daylight.

The whole next day, the flight, checking into the resort, the dinner on the beach, the subsequent sex before bed, I looked for signs of Erik's plotting, some hint of distaste, maybe even revulsion. I saw none. Erik seemed energized by me, our wedding, the ten-day trip to paradise. If Erik wanted me dead, he'd had plenty of opportunities before the wedding. As it turned out, we were a good couple: newlyweds, on our dream honeymoon. Aside from the thirty seconds of down stuffed into my face the night before, I should have been the happiest person on earth.

Since exchanging vows, Erik and I have had sex each and every night. Literally. And we're over seven months in. Not a record, I'm sure, but it's not like we have to use it up before we die. The weird thing is, Erik just assumes we're going to do it, like it's as gentlemanly to give it to your wife as it was to *not*

give it to your virgin fiancée. If it wasn't me living my life—if I were witnessing it from the outside—I'd think it was hilarious the way Erik washes up and brushes his teeth for me, then lays out his pajamas on the bureau for after. In fact, I've gotten Erik's sex routine down as succinctly as I've learned to predict his pillow trysts: At 11:30, the news ends and Erik switches off the TV, and within seconds, I hear the faucet in the bathroom. Then the toilet flushes just before the light goes out and he emerges. The toilet is my cue to get undressed, though I keep my pajama bottoms on most nights, make Erik maneuver his way around them. By midnight—and this is with a ten-minute bathroom routine—the deed is done and Erik is asleep. Right around two, I'll wake again, right as the pillow descends.

I've read somewhere that people become so conditioned by their alarm clocks that they wake up a split second beforehand, just so they can turn it off and avoid the clatter. I've gotten like that with Erik's attacks. I wake just as he stirs, positioning myself flat on my back, and wait for it to end. If I can, I take a deep breath, just in case. But I never need it. Erik's just not going to murder me. Of that, I am certain.

When Erik tried to murder me again the second night of our honeymoon, my degree of panic waned considerably. I didn't bolt out of bed when he was done, staying awake for only ten minutes after. I still didn't sleep very well, but again, I knew if he'd wanted to kill me, he could have—Erik's 6' 2", 210 pounds, and I'm a hundred pounds in a jacket. As the honeymoon rolled on, I became less and less disturbed by his attacks each night, taking diligent notes on their nature. By the sixth night, I was able to predict the timing, two hours to the minute after he drifted off. He did throw me on one occasion, when he was a half-hour late; I found out the next day, on a whale-watching cruise, he'd had trouble dozing off—something he'd eaten—but he pretended to be asleep because he didn't want to bother me. If he only knew.

The first time I ever had sex was with a guy my dad fought with in Vietnam. One night, when I was a freshman in high school, Dad announced that his buddy from the Corps was coming to visit. This didn't faze me, but I could tell my mother didn't like it. She sculpted her mashed potatoes, and when my dad wouldn't stop talking, getting graphic about killing and the bodies and the bureaucracy, Mom excused herself, starting the dishes and forgetting the banana pudding in the fridge.

The next day, four hours later than he was supposed to, this guy Jackson showed up at our house. Not only that, but he was all messed up, burns on his face and neck, and in place of his arms, two prostheses, complete with working hooks. He wasn't alone, either. Jackson brought an assistant, an older man, who I think was his nurse. For over a week, the three of them—my dad, Jackson, and the nurse (who was never introduced to us, so I don't know his name)—went down to the basement, closing the door behind them. They drank, told stories, played pool. My dad had always cussed a lot, but nothing like what I heard through the heating vents. Everything Jackson said was ten times worse. Mom and I could hear them, even over the TV turned all the way up. By the end of the week, she'd had it. When my dad stumbled up that night for bed, Mom met him in the hallway and laid down the law—the guests would be leaving first thing after breakfast. Jackson heard her, too, I was certain, because as soon as my mother stopped talking, the three men laughed. I was happy they'd be going—I knew Mom would win out—and planned on sleeping in, right through breakfast. Jackson and his manservant would be gone and our house would return to normal.

About an hour after my mother's decree, I woke to find Jackson sitting on the edge of my bed, patting my hair with one of the hooks and staring at my mouth. His slick lips quivered like he was still burning alive. He smiled at me, and at first, I thought he was trying to say good-bye, like we'd had some sort of connection. As soon as I opened my mouth to respond, my dad's old war buddy put one of his hooks into my throat, the other up to his lips, whispering *Shhhh*. Jackson then hooked back the covers, peeled my nightshirt up, and swung his legs over.

The whole thing was over in less than a minute, but before he could work his way off, Jackson's assistant, the nurse, burst through my door and tackled Jackson, covering his mouth so nobody would hear him scream. The nurse man then beat Jackson and beat him hard. Jackson got him a couple of times with his hooks, but before long, Jackson was limp and being dragged out of the room by his ankles. The nurse bowed to me before he shut my door, as if signing some unspoken agreement. I wondered if he knew he was too late.

When I came downstairs in the morning, late like I'd planned, my parents were cleaning out the garage, no one else around. None of us ever mentioned the time with Jackson to each other again, not until a few years later, when Jackson died and my father told us over dinner. I said I didn't remember him, which they seemed to believe. Every once in a while I think about him, and sometimes, I think that I imagined the whole thing, my own little secret with myself.

I meet a man at a motel outside of town every Friday evening at 5:30, when Erik and his entire office go out to TGI Friday's for light beers and Buffalo wings. It's not the same man every week that I have sex with, either. In the nine weeks I've been doing this, I've had one repeat and that was by accident—I didn't even remember the guy until he said something, halfway through, when it would have been more of a hassle for me to have him stop. Finding the guy is easy—I'm more than just attractive and no guy I've ever met is all that picky. I just go to the adult bookstore and wait. Lots of guys stop there on the way home from work, stocking up for the weekend, and all I have to do is walk down the same aisle, seem interested in the same movie, and before you know it, we're leaving together. The motel is just across the parking lot, enclosed by the same tall, orange fence as the bookstore, and by now, the woman in the office knows me, has a clean room set aside. The men are always more than happy to pay and are always quick finishers. Most of them try to set up something for another day, which never happens. A few have even tried to pay me, just assuming. I don't ever take the money—once a guy offered a thousand dollars—because that would be crossing a line. I just decline whatever they're holding out and ask them to leave. The best part is peeking through the curtains and seeing how many of them go back to the bookstore to buy the porn they'd set out for in the first place, the adventure of me not enough to hold them over. So far, it's been eight for nine, the one exception being the repeater, who wasn't too happy when I threatened to kill him if he ever tried to pick me up again. I was just blowing smoke, of course, but it's not like he knew that.

By instinct one night, while Erik was on top of me, doing his thing, I asked him to choke me. It wasn't something I'd planned or something I'd thought of, and it was definitely not something I wanted. But I asked him. He was in the phase of sex where he was holding off, trying to wait for me, a five-to-seven-minute stretch where he just coasted, worked with the rhythm, and most of all, looked me in the eye—I liked that part. This coasting segment of our relations was a good time for me, and one night a week, maybe every other week, if I had to be honest, I came. For real. With Erik.

The other nights, the comeless nights, I let Erik think he'd done his deed, fulfilled his purpose as a husband and a man. Otherwise, five-to-seven-minute stretches aren't enough to do the trick. Sometimes he's close but I'm not, so I give up and start with the acting job, let him move things along so we can get to sleep. On other nights, it's just not going to happen, no matter how long Erik pumps away. Remember, we do it every night, and even an old get-around like me isn't in the mood that much. Not anymore.

So one night, the five-to-seven-minute stretch over and me kind of bored, I waited until Erik got the face that tells me he's ready, moved into the final phase of the act, and then I said it: *Choke me.* His muscular forearms pushed down on either side of my face—it would have been easy, one hand on my throat, just a little pressure, something to make me gag a bit, if anything a change of pace. When he didn't seem to hear me— eyes closed at this point and getting his train getting pretty close to the station—I said it again: *Choke me.* This second time, Erik heard. Right as he emptied himself into me, his eyes opened, his mouth, too, and if he hadn't been so close, he for sure would've jumped off, probably cowered in the corner next to his shoe tree under the coat rack. Of course, when he did get off, Erik wanted me to repeat what I'd said, bewilderment filling him like he was the one who'd been fucked, and I denied saying anything. He asked several times more as he dressed in his pajamas, once more after the light went off, convinced as he was going to be. I wondered if this request would alter the sleepsmothering he would give me later, and I stayed awake for the two hours that night, anticipating. But two hours later, Erik woke, grabbed his pillow, and for thirty seconds, tried to murder me in the same old way, briefly and without conviction.

One night in high school, I went out with a guy named Dennis. I didn't know him except to see him in the hallways, but he asked me out and I said yes. This was at least two years after the Jackson incident, and by that point, I'd been with about a dozen guys from my school. Then, I wouldn't have said the high school me had a reputation, but now I know I did. Guys you don't know named Dennis don't ask you out unless they think they have good odds. I wasn't smart, wasn't active in clubs, and didn't have nice clothes or a car. I was just the girl who was pretty and willing. A lot of the other girls did the deed, but a dozen different guys since sophomore year? That was serious fucking for a girl my age.

After a movie, Dennis asked if I wanted to go to the Ravine, his voice breaking like he was going to cry, and when I said yes, Dennis' Nova moved up a gear. The Ravine was what we all called the local Forest Preserve that overhung the river. Everyone in my school used it to make out because at the time the cops didn't know about it, didn't break up the action. Dennis and I drove in and parked as far away from the other cars as we could. Then Dennis said he didn't want to stay in the car. He said he had something to show me, that he wanted to go down to the actual ravine. Kids in cars peppered the lot—everyone there for the same thing—so the request sounded strange. It was funny, what boys did, what they thought they had to do. I'd figured the hard part was asking about the Ravine, if I wanted to go. Once I said yes, everything after was easy. But Dennis seemed to think he still had work to do, to show me something on the trail. Even then, I was a sucker for effort. We headed into the darkness.

When we got to the end of the trail, there was a wooden railing lining the edge that overlooked the river. The railing was new—I hadn't been on the trail since Girl Scouts, maybe fourth or fifth grade. I pulled free of Dennis' hand and ran ahead, looking over the bar. It was dark, but I could still see the current, the darkness sliding downstream, slick and loud as it banged against the rocks, the moon drowning in the middle.

I turned around and saw that Dennis' pants were around his knees and he was coaxing his hand up and down a small penis. At the time, rape wasn't something they talked about in schools, wasn't something my mother had warned me about, was never a plot on a TV show. I knew what it was from firsthand knowledge, but really, I didn't think I had anything to be afraid of: I was going to do whatever Dennis wanted, so what could go wrong? I smiled at my date and lifted up my shirt, a white top with spaghetti straps and a tiny bow in the center. I folded the shirt over the railing and unbuttoned the snap on my jeans. Before I could unzip, Dennis finished. He grunted like all the boys grunted, his jism disappearing into the dark, his knees spreading and bobbing like a sick bird's. Then he lifted his pants up and refastened, staring at me the whole time, down at my breasts. I knew he had never seen any before and I considered myself special, somehow, even after what he'd just done.

"I don't know whether I should feel flattered or left out," I said then, those exact words. I remember because they sounded so cool, something an adult would say in a movie, the perfect comeback to Dennis' punchline. I assumed we would still do the normal thing, that he was seventeen and would be ready again in a snap.

Dennis didn't think I was witty, though. I'd never been tackled before, but with a head start, Dennis shoved me into the railing, my bare back hitting hard, a horizontal bruise across my torso already in the works. Worse, the railing wasn't that sturdy and I could feel the posts lift. I thought we might go over the edge, that we'd die together, people thinking we were lovers, that we were tragic. We didn't fall. Instead, Dennis grabbed my shirt and tried to pull it over my head, to dress me, a first in my experience. I finally was convinced that something was not right and tried to get away, my eyes on the trail, thinking it a magic portal to safety. I'd had guys get rough, go on when I said stop, one taking seconds when I didn't want to give. But nobody had ever hit me before, not even Jackson with his hooks, his charred skin, and his cigarette stink. Dennis just smelled like the woods, like pine and the river and a rage I didn't think I deserved.

I managed to squirm away, hoping to outrun him to the parking lot and find a familiar car—there were always a few—and someone to take me home. But Dennis pulled me to the ground by my hair, dragged me back toward the railing, rolling me to the point where my feet dangled off the edge. I thought I was going to go over, that Dennis was going to kick me right into the river, the rocks cracking me to pieces, my body floating downstream. It was going to hurt, I thought, my face hitting the shale, and it was going to be cold. I was going to be dead, murdered by crazy Dennis, whom I'd only met that day by my locker.

Dennis ran off down the trail instead, not kicking me to my death. I couldn't believe it, with how angry he was, that he'd found the restraint. Maybe he realized he'd get caught—my mother had met him when he picked me up—and the cops would have sweated him down, found my shirt in the dirt. Or maybe he'd heard something, somebody coming down the trail, and just got smart. But Dennis stopped, so close to murdering me. For that, I was grateful, and never told anyone, not that night, not when I saw him Monday at school, snickering at me, staring at my chest and whispering to his pals.

My therapist thinks I should wake Erik. I need to tell him what he's doing to me, just in case there's an accident. She thinks Erik could slip, or maybe, if he dreams the right dream, carry the sleepmurder out to its end. She asks me every time I lay myself down on her couch, reminding me again when I'm heading out her door. She makes good money off me, she jokes, three sessions a week, and would hate to lose the income. But I know she's serious. She wants me to tell him.

That my therapist wants me to take charge is no surprise. Before I started seeing her, I knew the simple solution—everybody in therapy does. I didn't need to go to a shrink to tell me that I should wake Erik, to remind me I was playing Russian roulette each and every night. The thing is, my therapist, Ellen, left a husband of thirty years the day she found him cheating. She tells the story—at least once a week—of how she saw him drive by, something tiny and blond in his lap, licking his neck, her shirt crumpled up on her shoulders. In one swift motion, Ellen pulled out her cell, called their lawyer, and asked him to refer her to a divorce attorney. The lesson here is that she's worth not even thinking about forgiving him. To consider staying with a man who cheats on you after thirty years is an insult to yourself, even if you do it for a second. She was strong, and I, too, could be strong.

I didn't start seeing Ellen because of Erik's sleepwalking. I was there for the other stuff, Jackson, Dennis, the men at the motel. Ellen, being the strong woman she is, thinks taking control of my sexuality isn't nearly as bad as my husband trying to kill me. For a few sessions, I corrected Ellen, telling her Erik does not try to kill me, that I've survived over two hundred attacks without as much as a scratch. But I stopped, because Ellen doesn't believe that, talks past it. Ignores it. This pisses me off more than anything, how she steers the conversation toward what she thinks is wrong with me. Who's paying who, anyway?

Ellen's fantasy is for Erik to come to her office with me, to work out our problems as a family. In other words, Ellen wants Erik to come in and for me to tell him what he does in our bed. This isn't going to happen. Erik thinks I see Ellen to overcome phobias—spiders, heights, tight places. I have those problems, too, but that's not why I'm seeing someone. If he came in, not only would I have to tell Erik about his pillow games, but Ellen would eventually want me to tell him about the other men, come clean on my whole life. Fucking brilliant advice, at $155 an hour.

A few months into therapy, I tracked down Ellen's ex, a city councilman I'd voted for in the previous election. I followed him around town, City Hall, the cleaners, Panera. At Sears, I pulled the porno shop maneuver, checked out the same long-life flashlights he was examining, bent over the right way, made the right amount of eye contact. It was a Wednesday morning, so the woman in the motel office was surprised to see me, but in a pleasant way. She was careful, like she always is, not to let on I'm a regular, Ellen's ex lingering right behind. In bed, he was pretty forgettable, but really, knowing Ellen, I expected no less.

Of course, I didn't tell her about him in therapy that afternoon, twisted revenge not the point. It's something about her and me that I know and she doesn't, my favorite thing in the whole world.

Before Erik ever put a pillow in my face, he took my virginity. Or so he thought. I remember that night in the Hilton, me unhooking my wedding dress, Erik frantic in the room, lighting candles, looking for a romantic music station on the TV, arranging the champagne on the nightstand. I was already drunk from the reception—rum-and-diets every half-hour—but I knew that this night needed to be special. We'd been waiting for this, both of us, the longest I'd gone, since my first time, without sex.

Even after all those months, Erik offered to skip it. Naked, pent up, and nervous, he said we could kiss, maybe give each other massages, even open the gift envelopes, which were down in the car locked in the trunk. I had to be careful, not to be too forward, to carry out the lie, to act afraid. I suggested he help me out of the dress, which he did, and start with the massage. When his fingers first hit my bare flesh, I faked a jolt, pulled away from him, acted violated. He slowed down after that, peeling off layer after layer of my virgin costume, folding them and placing them neatly on the dresser, like he would with his pajamas every night of our marriage.

When Erik got to the veil, I asked him to leave it on, to keep the mesh over my face. He didn't mind. I wondered if he thought I was bashful or just a bit kinky. He didn't ask. He just moved ahead, stripped me bare, and positioned himself on top. When he went in, I gritted my teeth, squeezed my eyes shut, faked a cough, all before relaxing, and, eventually, taking charge, as much as I could without giving myself away. Within fifteen minutes we were asleep, and two hours later, the pillow came down.

Regardless of the fact I wasn't a virgin, Erik thought I was and treated me like one. And I let him. To this day, I consider my wedding night with Erik the best night of my life, just like any good girl.

The night before our first anniversary, Erik surprises me. When he comes out of the bathroom, he's not naked, and his pajamas are not draped over his arm. To my surprise, Erik is wearing those PJs, buttoned to the top. He looks as if he's just done something wrong, an old dog who just pissed on the carpet despite knowing better. I'm waiting, of course, waiting for him to mount me so I can go to sleep, but I sense this isn't going to happen. Erik walks over, glancing a few times at my body, my top exposed and the rest of me under the comforter, then sits at the end of the bed. He does not say anything, and for a moment I wonder, different scenarios running through my head: Erik saw my car at the motel. Erik found out about the other men. Erik caught himself trying to kill me. All of them are possible, but none seem obvious. I try to ascertain, from Erik's posture, his sighing, his brooding, what could have happened. Impotence? Maybe something he's discovered in the bathroom. I've used condoms with every one of my motel men, but I consider the possibility that I—that we—have contracted something. Everything I think of seems life-changing, like the life I have with Erik is about to be altered, drastically, forever. Erik might be dying, I think. A lump. Bad news about a blood test, his physical at work the week before. Cancer, or something just as bad. Worse, a combination of any of the above: Erik saw my car at the motel on the way home from finding out he has cancer.

"I'm a little tired," he says. "Maybe we could just go to sleep tonight?"

I assume Erik is going to say something else. *Maybe we could just go to sleep tonight ... because I have cancer and VD and you're a whore and a liar*. I wait for a reason, but none comes. "Good night," Erik says and stretches across the bed, falling asleep and leaving me, exposed and terrified, next to him, alone.

I don't know what angers me more, that Erik didn't wait for an answer or that he asked the question in the first place. One day, I know I'll admit it's because he asked, but for now, I'm content in believing it's because he didn't wait for the answer, that him breaking our routine after so long came down to a rhetorical question. Erik's snoring makes me even madder, but if I know anything, once Erik starts snoring, he is asleep; there is no point in contesting his decision. It is 11:40 and Erik is gone to this world.

I find a nightgown at the bottom of a drawer, put it on, and twist off the lamp. I look at the clock and it reads 11:42. The nightgown feels strange to me since I've slept in just pajama bottoms every night since our wedding. Uneasy, I consider masturbating. I could keep the streak going on my own. I picture me doing just that and then Erik waking up. He'd feel guilty, never forgive himself, and things would be worse, change even more. By 11:45 I realize that I won't be able to go to sleep. Too many open ends exist. Too many changes, none of which I have any control over.

I assume the position I fall asleep in, but instead just lie there. I wait. I bide. I will not sleep, no matter how tired I am. I will not sleep, not at least until 1:40 a.m. The two hours will not pass quickly enough, me looking at the digital readout on the clock every minute, sometimes more than once during the same minute. But at 1:40, I can stop looking at the clock. Then we will see what it is I will do, what it is I decide.

# The Elephant in Our Bedroom

**N**ot too long ago, I won an elephant in a card game and now I keep him in our bedroom. As baffling as it seems, my wife hasn't said a word. It's been like that between us, not talking to each other, though if anything would induce conversation, I would've thought it would be the elephant in the corner of the room. But it hasn't come up, not the noise, the grocery bills, the leveled furniture, not even the shit, which, I have to admit, is pretty bad.

Once when we were newlyweds, I brought home a puppy, my wife disallowing it immediately. Renters, we couldn't have pets, nothing that breathed air, but there she was, a chocolate spaniel with a white spot over her left eye. The rest of the litter didn't have one and I was sold. I had already started calling her that, "Spot," during the two hours she spent in that old apartment, me laying newspaper and toweling pee. When my wife got home and saw what I'd done, it took her exactly three seconds to throw me out. Spot, too. She cited the landlord, my allergies, her lack of interest in loving something new. The man who gave me Spot took her back, saying her mark would save her, how someone else would think like I had. "Her brothers and sisters, maybe not. Might be the gunnysack and a tall bridge for them."

Instead of the elephant, I could have picked a '73 Dodge Charger, complete with new paint job, refabbed engine, twenty-inch chrome rims, even fuzzy dice, guaranteed to get any sixteen-year-old laid, but probably not me, twice as old and not nearly half as cool. Why the guy who lost the hand had an elephant, I don't know, but he said he could get one and I believed him. The next day, a truck arrived. The guy led the elephant off the back, smacking it in the ass with a reed, and when he asked where I wanted it, I said, "Bedroom." When the man suggested the back yard, maybe some sort of stable, I told him it was already October and my elephant didn't like the cold. "Whose does?" he said. I tore up the IOU and we shook on it. That's how I came to own an elephant. Later at the Kroger, I bought every head of lettuce in stock, plus a small bag of peanuts, just for fun. I figured my wife would make me get rid of it, anyway, my elephant, but as it turned out, the joke was on me.

I play games with my elephant when my wife is in the room, hoping she'll take notice, say something, something to initiate a dialogue. I toss my elephant lettuce and cucumbers and cabbages, my elephant catching them all with his trunk and stuffing the prizes into its mouth. I climb the trash can to the dresser and onto its back, then lumber from one side of the room to the other. After a few weeks, he learns how to grab me and place me up there itself, putting me back on the hardwood floor when he's had enough. Teaching him to stand on its hind legs has proven difficult, but we're working on it every day. Still, my wife does not mention any of it, bat an eye. She rubs moisturizer into her face, turns page after page of cheesy romances, pulls the covers higher over her head. Part of me thinks I should just bring it up, ask her straight out what she thinks of my elephant, of *our* elephant. But I don't. It's easier at the end of the day to let it go than force a discussion. Maybe we used to be the type of people who threw things in each other's face—Spot, for instance—but we're past that now. I like to think it's because we've matured, that we don't speak because we've reached a comfort zone, a point where we know what the other is thinking without having to say anything at all, like twins who finish each other's sentences, only with thoughts. But my wife ignoring the elephant doesn't seem much like progress, like some point in our relationship we should be proud of. Then again, what do I know? I might not know progress if it grabbed me by the neck and squeezed my head clean off.

I haven't named my elephant yet, just in case my wife does wake up and make me give it back. I wonder if I still remember Spot only because she was *Spot*, if a nameless pup would have been easier to let go. I imagine taking the elephant back, not to the man with the pair of queens to my three threes, but to the man with the spaniels from years ago. I picture this man draping a large sack over the elephant's ears and tusks and trunk, then rolling it over the guardrail of a tall bridge. I wonder if it would survive the fall, only to drown in the current. Elephants are enormous—you never realize how big till you have one in your bedroom with your wife—and you'd think they could survive something a dog or a person couldn't, some sort of sliding scale of survival, of ruggedness. Even without a name, the image of my elephant dying that way makes me cringe. I almost weep, it's such a miserable thought. I've lost so much already, everything much smaller, but falling from the same insurmountable height.

# B positive

*Movement amongst the trees of a forest shows that the enemy is advancing.*
                              —Sun Tzu, *The Art of War*

My right leg is caught in a bear trap on the outskirts of my grandfather's Montana estate. It is the estate where he will soon marry a girl sixty years his junior, a girl I used to be engaged to, the girl who will comfort him with amazing sexual escapades until his death, the girl who will no doubt inherit his vast fortune instead of me. My shinbone is shattered, the separated piece of leg hanging on by veins, tendons, and a few hairs. I feel no pain—not because losing Lallana to my eighty-year-old grandfather has left my heart like stone, but because Grandpop, upon setting the bear trap, left three syringes of morphine, along with a note reminding me I was *not* invited to the joyous event, that my current predicament is my own damn fault.

It is nearly nine in the morning, almost an hour before the ceremony, nearly half an hour since the trap snapped shut on my leg. Despite an amateur tourniquet, the blood is substantial. I have another hour—two, max—before death. Grandpop is not going to let this go that far, I'm assuming, but that assumption holds less and less water as my leg turns bluer and the grass grows blacker with my blood. Even before my first morphine injection, I'd expected Grandpop to appear, a crack team of physicians at his side, or for a hospital helicopter to land on the roof of the servants' quarters to whisk me away—Trapper John and Hawkeye waiting on the hillside in Hawaiian shirts, that sort of thing. But the luxury of time and the complete lack of physical sensation has gotten me to thinking: Why *three* vials of morphine when the first might last longer than I would? I asked this question nine minutes ago. It has been an uncomfortable nine minutes.

Along with the morphine and the lengthy rubber tube that serves as my tourniquet, Grandpop left me reading material. There is *The Art of War*, by Sun Tzu, a required text in my family, what Grandpop would read to me in the place of bedtime stories. Second is a copy of the restraining order filed against me by my ex-fiancée and soon-to-be step-grandmother, Lallana. The section stating, "… shall not come within one hundred feet of Ms. DuPree" is highlighted in pink fluorescence, coupled with a map of Grandpop's estate that details the less-than-one-hundred-foot proximity I now occupy. Lastly, there is the issue of *Playboy* that features Lallana, the love of my life, last year's Miss May. Her pictures have been altered, as Lallana is no longer nude, instead dressed in a digitally imposed wedding gown. Lallana still has that same sexy glare that made me fall in love with her, particularly the shots on and around the pinball machine. But I get the point. I would not have considered my grandfather to have much of a sense of humor, but then again, if I were about to marry and consummate with Lallana, I'd be in pretty high spirits, too.

A little after nine, I hear rumbling in the woods and hope it is not a bear. Irony of ironies: to be mauled by a bear while trapped in a bear trap; Darwin Awards, here I come. If I had the strength to unclasp the jaws from around my leg, I could crawl away, or better yet, reset the trap next to me, hoping the bear would somehow stumble into it on its way to eating me. Darwin Awards for bears? But I *don't* have the strength—bear traps, after all, are made to hold bears, not wounded soap opera actors. If a bear *is* coming, at least the morphine is still pumping through my veins; I could lie back at the edge of my seat as the bear tosses me around, waiting for it to slash something vital, maybe break my neck in a quick shake.

The rumbling in the woods is not a bear, but a man in a silk shirt with a couple of cameras around his neck and an aluminum ladder under his arm: paparazzi. I was hoping none of them would think of approaching Grandpop's estate from this angle, but it was inevitable. The paparazzo doesn't see me right away, his eyes glued to the tree line, looking for a low point to set up his ladder and get his money shot. Too bad he wasn't an hour earlier—then I would be the one to find *him* stuck in the trap. Of course, I would have left him to bleed, kicking his cameras as I passed, but fortunately for me, he won't know that when I ask him to call for help.

The paparazzo does not see me until he opens his ladder and one of the legs is about to come down on my groin. Insult to injury. When at last he notices me, he startles and falls backward, the ladder toppling to the ground. Within a microsecond, he's on his feet again and snapping away, zooming in and out, galloping around me like a wild bronco, hitting every angle of my face until he is out of film in both cameras.

"You're the grandson," the creep says. "The jilted daytime hunk." He loads film like most people put on deodorant, then resumes shooting. "How about a smile? My boss might like one with a smile."

This scumbag hasn't even noticed my leg caught in the trap.

"Joshua, isn't it?" the paparazzo says from behind the flashes. "My name's Mario."

"Jacob," I say. "My name is Jacob."

A paparazzi photo was how I found out about Grandpop and Lallana. I was down at the Ralph's, in the checkout line with a box cake, a half-dozen free-range chicken eggs, and a tub of frosting, set to bake my baby a cake for her nineteenth. Then

I noticed the tabloid cover, a fuzzy shot of Grandpop rubbing something into Lallana's shoulders next to an anonymous swimming pool. It was surreal. At first, I didn't even make the connection. I was staring at this beautiful girl in a bikini and sunglasses, thinking to myself, *Man, I hope I'm that lucky when I'm as old as that guy.* For like a minute, my mind was convinced that the photo wasn't of Grandpop, but of Burt Reynolds. *The Bandit's still got it*, I thought. *Loni Anderson, who needs ya?* Then I saw the tattoo, the *JG*—my initials—on Lallana's left ankle. I flipped. Literally, I fell face-first onto the grocery conveyor, smashing the eggs with my throat as the belt dragged me toward a deadly chokehold, my collar disappearing under the item scanner. Three bag boys had to wrestle me out of my shirt before I could run home and find out what the hell was going on.

Lallana just laughed and assured me that the photo was a fake, that 99 percent of what those rags printed was garbage.

I believed her. Why wouldn't I? Grandpop had looked and smelled like death for thirty years. I was hot and rich and famous. I ordered a cake from the bakery and forgot the whole mess.

The day after her birthday, for which I gave her a yellow Dodge Viper convertible, Lallana left and told me to forward her things to Grandpop's ranch. Her Dear Jacob note explained two things: 1) She was in love with my grandfather because he was ten times the man I'd ever be, and 2) I shouldn't kill myself, because, well, Lallana didn't explain why I shouldn't kill myself.

For a professional photographer, Mario's not very perceptive. He takes six rolls of me lying on the ground, four times kicking my nerve-dead leg as he goes by. This with bone shards scattered about the grass like croutons.

"You're the best, baby," Mario says. Six rolls seem to be enough, as he stops taking pictures, turning his energies toward smoking. He offers me one, which I gobble. "Usually, my subjects don't just lie there and let me plug at them like that. I mostly get back shots, people running away, giving me the finger, that sort of thing. But I think I've really captured your pain—or maybe your compulsion for forgiveness. That'll be up to the writers."

"I'm dying," I say. "My leg's caught in this bear trap and I'm steadily bleeding to death."

Mario winks. "Don't pull a Sean Penn on me, pal. You're in public, therefore, you're fair game." He redirects his attention to the hedge line, spying for a spot to set up his ladder.

"I need you to call an ambulance," I say. "I'm losing blood and will die without medical attention. There's a hospital fifteen minutes from here. If you hurry, you can make it. Tell them I'm B positive."

Mario drops his cigarette on the back cover of *The Art of War* and stamps it flat with the bottom of an alligator boot, probably faux. "Help me out here," he says. "Is the fence behind these trees electric? I hear a hum, so I'm thinking *yes*. But I don't want to find out the hard way."

What Mario doesn't know is that my dying body is blocking a secret passage through the fence, basically this little doggie door that gets you through the fence. It's the secret passage I used for sneaking out past curfew, the passage Grandpop uses to shake his security detail, the passage I was using when I tripped the bear trap. Farther down, Mario keeps setting up the ladder, climbing to the top and trying to take pictures. Hedges block his view. Even if he could find a clearing, the ceremony is nowhere near this part of the estate. This joker's best shot would probably be of a withered bison carcass—Grandpop's bleeding hooks are right though the bushes, hooks where he hangs his kills to dry for jerky. I half hope Mario falls into the fence—electric as lightning—except it'd be nice if he'd call an ambulance. He might be my only hope.

Worse, what used to be my ankle is starting to tickle: The first morphine shot is wearing off. In half an hour, without the next injection, the pain will become unbearable. I wait a few minutes until the tickles turn to twinge, then unscrew the second syringe and shoot up. It is instantly as if I don't have feet, legs, arms, anything. I'm almost glad my leg is cheese as I feel stupendous.

Mario returns, his ladder operation a bust, spying the needle leaving my skin. "What are you, some kind of junkie?" He shoots two more rolls of film, one of my face, asking me to roll my eyes, the other roll some close-ups of my arm and the morphine needle lying across my stomach. "This is great stuff. Thank you, my friend. My debtors thank you. My ex-wife thanks you. And if I had kids, they'd thank you, too."

Mario jogs off into the woods, cameras bouncing around his neck, ladder steady under his arm.

The blue in my leg grows past my knee and into my thigh.

I feel fucking fantastic—but in a melancholy sort of way.

"Here Comes the Bride" sings happily in the distance. Harps, Grandpop's favorite. It is just after ten. The ceremony has begun. Right now, a half dozen Playmates are a parade of velvet and cleavage, while Lallanna's theatrical agent walks her down the aisle. Grandpop stands at the altar with his best man, my little brother Blaine, whom I now call "Kiss-Ass Traitor." Forty very exclusive guests are turning their heads to see the lovely Lallana float across red silk, an angel with a dagger in her garter. I am not up in the organist's loft, as planned, banging on the glass.

The sound quality about the music changes, and after a moment of thinking I've died, I realize the electric fence has been shut down. The gate surrounding the secret passage opens and a man in a black suit and sunglasses approaches, carrying a large black leather bag. The man is Abraham Kootenay, my grandfather's head of security and lifelong best friend. He has come to rescue me.

Twenty-three years ago, Abraham, my godfather, held my mother's hand in the back of a limousine as she was rushed to the hospital, ready to deliver me if need be. Abraham taught me to play piano, wrote most of my English themes, bought me beer and condoms whenever I wanted, and when I was cut from my high school baseball team, took the coach for a drive and convinced him of the value of having a batting-practice fastball in his bullpen. As I lie bleeding to death in the grass, all he says is my name. My *nick*name: *Jake-O.* Not a good sign.

Inside Abraham's bag is a medical kit, including a bag of B positive the size and shape of a catcher's mitt. Abraham taps a vein in my left arm and inserts the needle. As if he's done it a hundred times, he connects the blood bag to the tube, turning it red, inflating my vein to blue. Instantaneously, my leg renews its vigorous bleeding. To remedy that problem, Abraham pulls a half dozen metal clamps out of the bag and proceeds to attach them to my stringy severed veins, pretty much stopping the flow. Before long, I feel stronger. Abraham puts his free hand on my shoulder as the bag empties into me, but when I look up at him and smile, he pulls his hand back and looks off into the woods.

"If a bear comes, and sooner or later, one will, given all this blood, aim between the eyes." Abraham reaches into the bag and drops a .44 magnum onto my chest. I know this weapon. It is the gun John Wayne gave Grandpop for his fiftieth birthday, a gun that's been dubbed "The Duke," the gun Grandpop hunts bear, elk, and moose with, a gun that will kill anything with an appetite big enough for me. Its barrel is longer than the piece of leg hanging off my shin, its bullets thicker than my thumb. I could probably use it as a club and hold my own.

The blood bag takes fifteen minutes to empty, then Abraham removes the needle, swabs the hole with alcohol, and Band-Aids the cotton ball to my arm.

"Abe," I say, but he interrupts me.

"I don't know what he's going to do with you, Jake. Don't ask me, because he hasn't told me. You just shouldn't have done that movie, Jake-O. You know, if it were up to me ...."

"How did she look?" I ask.

Abraham puts his hand back on my shoulder. "Can you feel the blood, Jake-O?"

"How did she look, Abe? Coming down the aisle—how did she look?"

"Awful," Abraham says. His eyebrow crinkles and I know he is winking at me behind his shades. "I'd rather blow a marmot than kiss that two-timer."

This breaks the ice, but it feels funny to laugh. Before I can ask anything else, Abe and his bag are through the gate. The electric hum of the fence returns, blocking out the distant buzz of applause and harp. "There Goes the Bride," whatever. Abe is weighing my life versus his pension.

For the first time in thirteen years, I have a grandmother. Not many twenty-three-year-olds can say that, and when you throw in the fact I've slept with her, the numbers would have to go way down.

There have been at least three characters in the history of soap operadom who have worn eye patches, two of them to great, lasting effect. Several actors—in the dawn of their twilight—have been resexified with a cane. Multiple personality disorder shows up more often than the Olympics, and amnesia is a lot like chicken pox: Everybody gets it at least once. So why not a young, compassionate, peg-legged surgeon with a taste for fast cars and even faster candy stripers? It could work.

Abraham's portable blood bank has reconvinced me that Grandpop has no intention of letting me die, but the foul state of my leg suggests he's willing to leave his mark. When I look at the piece of my body threatening independence, I can't imagine anything short of a blue parking tag. An update:

My foot? No way. I am now a monoped.

The shin? That's shattered. No such thing as half a shin.

The knee? Unlikely. I wonder if I'd need the knee for those artificial legs, the ones that let you play basketball and run in the handicapped Olympics.

My thigh? Maybe.

My balls? I try not to think about what might happen to my balls.

While trying not to think of my balls, I sense another rustling in the bushes and again hope it's not a bear. This time, at least, the Duke sits at my side. I wait for the noise to emerge, aiming the handheld cannon in the general direction of a large tree with many armlike branches and clawlike buds. When the noisemaker is slow to appear, I grow nervous and check the chamber. What I see again makes me less than confident: Only one bullet sits between me and 1,600 pounds of hungry. It's a good thing for me that bears do not hunt in packs. I roll the chamber back in and repoint the gun into the woods.

My newest visitor is not a bear, not even close, instead a beautiful young brunette in a slinky black dress and high heels. She is magnificent, majestic, and awe-inspiring. She also has a hard time walking. Finding footing among the twigs and soft earth appears to be a challenge for her as she falls on her face twice before making it five feet. Even better, each time she stumbles, her breasts find their way out of her dress, but without moving, as if suspended by a second, invisible dress. The Duke returns to my side while I watch the woman struggle, a true splendor in the grass.

"You're Jacob Galvisten, aren't you?" the woman says when she finally makes her way to my side.

She's almost as beautiful as Lallana. I nod.

The woman's expression turns narcotic. "I knew it was you! I used to watch *Forever Yours* every morning. You're a hunk—a hunk's hunk!"

"Guilty as charged," I say. "What's your name?"

"Dawn," the woman says. "Dawn D'Armani."

Dawn D'Armani tiptoes around my leg and puddle of blood, sheltering her eyes as if the whole mess were the sun. For a second, she steps out of sight and I think she's gone through the secret passage, but then I sense soft, silky skin against my face and look up to see black lacy panty and half of a heart tattoo on each inner thigh; Dawn's seated behind me and her legs are wrapped around my head.

"Wow, *the* Jacob Galvisten—right here between my very own legs!" she says, squeezing and giggling as if my head were a birthday present. "By the way, what happened to your foot?"

"I got it caught in this bear trap," I say. It is an obvious answer, but I think I'm dealing with an obvious answer-type person.

"You're not even a bear," Dawn D'Armani says. "Why would you go and do a thing like that?"

"I didn't," I say, but Dawn's adoring attention seems to want more information. "My grandfather did it to me. He caught me trying to break up his wedding and steal his wife so I can marry her myself."

"That's kind of gross," Dawn D'Armani says. "You want to marry your grandmother?"

"She's not my real grandmother. My real grandmother died with my parents in a plane crash when I was nine. It was a real big story. Maybe you remember it?"

"No," Dawn D'Armani says. "I wasn't in that plane crash."

Dawn's legs remove themselves from my cheeks as she stands, which my mind tells me is a bad thing. Even on the morphine, I could smell her perfume all around me. It made me forget about my leg and the ever-growing possibility of my death, if for just a moment.

"It sounds like you and your grandfather really hate each other," Dawn D'Armani says.

"I never hated my grandfather, not until he stole my fiancée. After my parents died, my grandfather raised me. He's a famous actor, too, you know, more famous than me. One of the greats of all time. Better than Olivier or Burton. Brando, too, he'd say, but he and Brando used to argue about that all the time."

"Is Brando your old fiancée?" Dawn D'Armani asks.

Dawn D'Armani grows more and more adorable by the second. "Not really," I say. "But anyway, my grandfather only stole my fiancée because I once played him in a movie, a parody kind of thing, making fun of him when he was my age, how some people thought he was a little cocky."

"That doesn't sound too bad. I bet that was real funny."

"I won an Oscar for it—it was my first movie."

Dawn D'Armani claps and smiles, kicking her feet up in the air as if I've just made a free throw or scored the winning touchdown. "Your grandfather should be proud of you."

"That's what I thought. But he's never won an Oscar, just nominated—six times. Before he died, Brando brought that up all the time—he'd won twice. Anyway, now my grandfather hates me and is probably going to kill me."

"Kill?" Dawn D'Armani says. "You should give your Grandpop more credit. Try to think positive, be more optimistic."

Immediately, I know what's going down: I never once referred to Grandpop as "Grandpop" to Dawn in our short conversation.

"Why did he send you?" I say.

Dawn looks down at me for a second, then falls into the grass, her airbrush-perfect breasts escaping again, landing just inches from my fingertips. "Why did *who* send me?" she asks, extra-slowly to replace herself in her dress.

"Cut the crap. How much is the old man paying you?"

Dawn D'Armani stands up, fixing her dress and pushing hair back from her eyes. "Too much. I would have done it for less." Dawn's speech pattern changes, from distant glare to pretty sharp. "I really did watch you every day and really did want to meet you."

"Well, here I am. Now go call me an ambulance or you'll watch me die."

Dawn D'Armani looks away. "I can't do that, cutie pie."

"No?" I'm not surprised. "What are you *supposed* to do?"

"Keep you distracted. If I liked you well enough, ask you to marry me, you know, get your mind off your new grandma. So, what do you say?"

Dawn's bubbly ditz routine is gone, but the bod is not. And I actually like her better with something upstairs besides collagen. "Tempting," I say. "But I'm in love with my grandmother."

"That's still kind of gross," Dawn says. "And I'm real sorry that I can't call an ambulance. But I will tell you this: I've met the old man. He doesn't seem like the kind of guy who would kill his own grandson over a little statue."

I look down at the bear trap and my soon-to-be stump.

Dawn smiles. "Gotta go," she says, and gets on her hands and knees to crawl through the doggie flap. "The dancing will start soon. William Hurt is in there somewhere, and besides, I honestly don't want be around here to see what happens next."

Eight years of living with Grandpop and six years of dealing with agents, producers, and critics haven't taught me shit about life, nothing besides one basic truth: "Life is hard." I want to think that Grandpop, in his really messed-up view of things, is trying to teach me that truth here with this bear trap, that he's pouring Nietszche on my wounds and not giving me anything to bite down on. Life is hard—for everyone except the great Jeremiah Galvisten.

Once again, the hum of the electric fence disappears as someone is coming through the gate. The loss of blood—even with the transfusion—has made me weak, and the clamps aren't foolproof. I hope Abraham has returned, with more blood, a stretcher, or even news of Grandpop's surprising and sudden annulment.

It is not Abraham.

It is my grandfather.

I raise the Duke and point it at his head, directly between the eyes.

"Damn it, put the Duke down," Grandpop says. "I told Kootenay to give you a forty-four, but not the Duke, goddamnit. I just might have to shoot that bastard when I'm done here with you."

I cock the hammer.

"You couldn't hit me if I put the barrel in my mouth," Grandpop says. He gets off his hands and knees and walks toward me with a white cane twirling in front of him, spinning it around his finger like a biplane rotor. It's a trick he picked up doing *Love, Lies, and Bleeding*, his second Oscar nomination, a loss to Ernest Borgnine, the one defeat of the six that he hates the most. "Borgnine," he'll say. "Goddamn-Marty-McHale-TV-hack-fat-shit."

"Don't come near me, you crazy S.O.B.," I say, wondering to myself what I'd do if he advanced. But my hand has been raised too long, holding what feels like a cement block instead of a large firearm. The Duke, along with my hand, falters.

Grandpop comes closer. He is wearing a tuxedo, all white—the shirt, vest, tie, shoes, spats, and top hat, matching his white hair, mustache, and beard, and contrasting with his unnaturally golden brown tan. He looks like fried chicken slathered in mayonnaise. I think that perhaps I've died—and that Grandpop is God.

I know that I'm alive, however, when Grandpop smacks me across the forehead with his cane and kicks the Duke out of my hand. I cannot feel anything, but I can watch my left eye go blind, blood filling the socket like water in a sink.

Grandpop struts laps around my perimeter, spinning the cane, spouting Sun Tzu mantras: "*Hold out baits to entice the enemy. Feign disorder, and crush him*," he says. "And you're easily enticed, Mr. One-Facial-Expression-Fits-All."

The Duke lies just a yard away, but too far away to reach. I try scooching myself closer, but can't make it all the way, the bear trap holding me in place.

"*The clever combatant imposes his will on the enemy, but does not allow the enemy's will to be imposed on him*," Grandpop cites. He looks around on the ground then lifts a white shoe and pushes the toe into the last syringe of morphine, crushing the glass and spraying his spats with the precious, precious drug. If I'm out here much longer, my leg *will hurt*.

"Are you going to kill me?" I ask. Half of me—the bottom half—hopes he says "yes."

"That's an interesting question, Jake-O," Grandpop says. "But I'd have to answer 'no.'"

"I was in love with her," I say. "I still am."

Grandpop stops pacing and stares into my eyes. I've seen this look before, the same look he has when he's about to take a kill shot. I then picture Lallana gently stroking my face—my head mounted on the wall above her and Grandpop's fireplace.

"You wouldn't know what love is," Grandpop says, and kicks what used to be my leg. Surprisingly, I feel it. Neither tickle nor twinge, either, but pain—really, really intense pain. I think of the third syringe of morphine giving the worms the time of their lives.

"What about you?" I say. I pick up a pine cone and throw it, missing him by four feet. "Do you even love Lallana?"

Grandpop stops and stares into the air. There is nothing there except a small plane, which disappears into a bank of dark clouds. Grandpop resumes his pacing and screaming. "I can't believe you were on a soap opera. A Galvisten! I'm glad I never won an Oscar."

Behind Grandad, I see the bushes rustle and stop, then rustle again. Grandpop goes on about having raised me the right way, about duty, honor, and family, and how I'm a disgrace to the Galvisten name, how I should have been more like my kiss-ass traitor brother, Blaine, who probably sucks Grandpop's cock more often than Lallana.

"I wonder what your parents would say if they saw what you've become."

Grandpop does not see or hear the bear. The birds sense it first, flying free, then the rustling starts. A few branches part, and after a moment's calm, a grizzly emerges and heads toward us with intent, running much too fast for so much weight. I can only see its face, its eyes and teeth, within the brown. It's like the forest has come alive and this bear is its harbinger, the ferocity unlike anything I've ever seen. Before Grandpop can turn his head, the bear is upon him, engulfing him, knocking him to the ground with one swipe of its paw, leaving a print across Grandpop's white back, the rips in his jacket seeping red.

"Goddamn it!" Grandpop says, but relatively calmly, as if he'd just locked his keys in his car. "Jake, shoot this bear between the eyes so we can settle this man to man."

I do not move. Grandpop looks over to see the gun out of my, and his, reach. The bear falls on top of him and he disappears under the mass of fur and horrible stench.

"Grab that fucking gun!" Grandpop yells from underneath the pile.

The bear and Grandpop roll around. The bear has Grandpop's right hand in its mouth, rips it off at Grandpop's wrist. Grandpop gives the bear its money's worth, too, poking at its eyes with the cane. The bear—more annoyed about its eyes than Grandpop seems to be about his missing hand—lets go and makes for Grandpop's head. Grandpop ducks down and, in true Grandpop style, bites the bear in the nuts, not letting go until he's able to rip off a significant amount of tissue.

With a rush of adrenaline, I make a last-ditch grab at the Duke. To my surprise, I am able to reach it, clutch it in my hand, my finger on the trigger and ready to shoot whatever I decide needs dying. As a child, I pictured holding it, shooting at all kinds of things, bears and people included, though not at the same time, certainly not my grandfather. Even though I know what I'll see, I open the barrel to look at the single shot: five more rounds have not magically appeared. I close the barrel then notice blood squirting in the air. I look back at the bear trap: I have ripped the bottom portion of my leg completely off. The bleeding has resumed at record pace, all of Abraham's clamps popped free. Of course, once I realize what's happened, the pain is unlike anything a person can imagine, could act out in a movie.

"Shoot him, Jake!" Grandpop yells. Tiny pieces of the bear's furry scrotum fly from Grandpop's teeth. His white wedding duds are camouflaged with grass stains, mud, and grizzly fluids. "Aim between the eyes!"

I recock the hammer and make sure the lone bullet is in the chamber. Before I shoot, I ask, "Do you love her, Grandpop? Do you love Lallana?"

"Shoot the bear!" Grandpop says. "Shoot the goddamn bear!"

I do nothing. It may be because I lack the strength to aim the Duke and pull his trigger, but it's hard to say whether or not I would if I could. I watch the bear roll about on its back, roaring in a slathery rage and slapping at its lacerated sack with its hind claws, which can't make things any less painful for the bear.

Grandpop gets up and moves toward me. "Redeem yourself, boy. Shoot this bear right now."

Before Grandpop can reach me and do whatever he's planning, the bear tackles him from behind and goes for the neck. I'm guessing this is it, roll credits.

I raise the Duke just as the bear rises to its hind legs, towering over my Grandpop. The bear stands twelve feet tall but seems a hundred. After a second's pause to scream into the air, the bear dives onto Grandpop, claws slashing, fangs thrashing. Grandpop spins, teeth gnashing, fingers poking. Grandpop gets the worst of it, but does some damage of his own.

"Shoot the fucking bear, Jake!" he yells with what's left of his face.

The Duke's lone shot goes off.

I don't know who I've hit. As if I've rung a round bell, both the bear and Grandpop stop wrestling. A thin trickle of blood streams down from their hairy brown-and-white pile, oozing through the grass and bearprints, mixing in with my own syrupy life force. The pile of bear and Grandpop rises, then falls, rises, then falls again, a desperate gasp at either breath or escape. Given everything I've endured in my life, including the pain that gets worse every second, I have learned but one thing, much more than "Life isn't fair": You can poke a bear in the eyes, run away from it when it's hungry, even shoot a hundred of its cousins and dry their carcasses on hooks in your back yard. But no animal that size is going to sit back and let you bite off its nuts.

I still don't know which one I've hit, but it doesn't matter. Whoever emerges the victor is coming for me next.

# Dave Corzine Does Not Live Here

D ave Corzine does not live in my apartment. To my knowledge, he has never lived in my apartment, and since I live
in my apartment and will continue to live in my apartment, there are no plans for him to live in my apartment any
time soon.

Dave Corzine does not live in most people's apartments,
I'm sure. Dave Corzine, in fact, probably only lives in one
apartment: Dave Corzine's apartment, if such a thing exists.
And that, like most things, has nothing to do with me.

Actually, all of this has *everything* to do with me. The
fact Dave Corzine does not live in my apartment does not
prevent Dave Corzine from receiving twenty-five calls a week—
on average—at my number. In *my* apartment. Sometimes, it's
less, others, it's more. *Much* more. Since I don't receive any calls
myself, it doesn't really matter—*all* the calls I receive are for
Dave Corzine. I do not have friends and do not keep in touch
with any family. My phone number is unlisted, and I never give
it out when buying something. Once last April, I received a call
for a "Jonas," a wrong number, but it was only that one time.
Like I've said, all my calls are for Dave Corzine.

Given so much practice, I have perfected a response to
these Dave Corzine-seeking calls. It goes exactly like this:

Dave Corzine does not live here. Dave Corzine has never lived here. I don't know where you can find him. Someone has given you the wrong number. Please tell whoever gave you this number to stop giving out this number because Dave Corzine does not live here, nor anywhere you think this number dials into. I live here, alone, and I am not Dave Corzine. Good-bye and good luck in your search.

It does not work.

On most occasions, when I hang up, I can't take two steps away before the phone rings again, the same person I just hung up on calling and asking for Dave Corzine. I repeat my practiced response, and after a pause, the person reads my number from wherever they have it written down. I let them know that the number they have read is indeed the number they had dialed, but that the number does not connect them with Dave Corzine.

Again, they ask if Dave Corzine is there. Like I've been kidding.

Sometimes, as if I'm this Dave Corzine's secretary or some sort of telephone police, they explain that they're *supposed* to get hold of Dave Corzine; they tell me they're from a newspaper or a board of trustees or an agency, like that's going to make Dave Corzine magically appear. I repeat my practiced response yet again, only louder, then hang up, skipping the good-bye and good luck parts. After this, only about one out of every ten Dave Corzine callers calls back, persistent in their quest for Dave Corzine.

One out of ten is more than enough.

I am not the type of person who would know who Dave Corzine is. I live alone in a one-room apartment in Chicago, thirty-four blocks from the lake and twenty-three from downtown, my single window fifteen feet from the El tracks. I take the train into the suburbs, where I work in a one-room office for a company that suckers other companies' customers into buying extended warranties on electronic goods. By the time these customers get to me, the store these saps have bought their electronics from has gone under, so the saps want to kill someone the second the batteries in their remote go dead. On Mondays, Wednesdays, and Fridays, I work behind the counter from eight until twelve, dealing with in-person complaints. From one until five, I answer the phone, usually telling callers to bring their broken gizmo down to our office, where I'll see them again later that week, recognizing their voice, their complaint, their broken good.

On Tuesdays and Thursdays, I answer phones in the morning and work the counter in the afternoon.

The company designed this schedule, I've guessed, to keep its employees alert. To keep our productivity level at its highest. And possibly, in the most bright-eyed of perspectives, to keep us happy.

It does not work.

Despite my company's attempt at making my life more palatable through their routine break of routine, I look forward to no day of the week in particular, nor do I dread one part of the day as opposed to the other. On most days, I am not able to cite which day it is, or whether or not I've eaten lunch or had either of my breaks. If a person I'm talking to either on the phone or at the counter asks me what day or time it is, I want to tell them to plug their broken DVD player into the wall outlet and find out. If the clock's what's broken, they're screwed. I only tell them whether or not—and usually *not*—my company will give them money to replace or fix—usually fix—their electronic good. It does not matter to me if the person is satisfied with my answer or if they wish my company bankruptcy and me a lonely, painful death. I don't care.

And this is the key to dealing with people for a living, I've found: not caring. It's why I've been able to avoid getting fired, why I can wrestle myself out of bed and into clothes every day, why I have not vocally or physically harmed a customer, and why I haven't yet dived onto the El tracks and taken a bite out of the third rail. Suicide would be an answer—if I cared.

But, as I've mentioned, I don't.

Nettendorf, the person who works the schedule opposite mine, does not care, either. Nettendorf—the only name I know him by, the name I read off his nametag—is, however, better at hiding his lack of care than I am. Nettendorf says "Good day" and "Good luck" when on the phone, adding a smile when at the counter. Occasionally, when a rendezvous with a client goes exceptionally well, Nettendorf will utter the word "Bliss." Maybe he uses this word to replace "Oh, yes!" or "All right!" or maybe he just thinks he's some kind of smart-ass. I can't tell which. But the only word I hear from him when we are alone is "Bliss."

And that's one word too many.

Nettendorf's hiding of his non-caring puts him above me in the company's eyes, I think, as Nettendorf is given preference when it comes to choosing vacation time each December. In actuality, this is the kind of favoritism that also makes him my superior, although nothing changes the fact he does the exact same thing I do—only at opposite times. I assume Nettendorf makes more money than I do, but I cannot confirm this suspicion. Nettendorf and I do not speak about such things. In some ways, Nettendorf's uncanny ability to express disingenuous care makes me nauseous. In others, it makes him my idol: If I could care as much—or as little—as Nettendorf, at the same time as Nettendorf, while making as much money as I assume Nettendorf makes, then Nettendorf, my job, and my life, would be more tolerable.

But, for now, that's not the situation.

The week before Christmas, Dave Corzine receives eighty-one calls at my apartment. This is the record for calls received at my apartment in one week, and these calls are only the p.m. calls. I cannot account for the calls that come in while I'm at work, at the market, or in the shower. My only recourse in the Dave Corzine matter is that I am a heavy sleeper, and not even calls coming into my apartment for Dave Corzine can wake me. For this I am grateful. If only I could sleep all the time.

Instead of returning to work after lunch the Monday after this record-setting Dave Corzine call week, I take the train back to the city and walk sixteen-and-a-third blocks to the nearest public library. I put the name "Dave Corzine" into the library's computosearch and find no books that are by or about Dave Corzine. After an hour's wait, I get onto the Internet and log the name "Dave Corzine" into a search engine. Four hundred and seventy-two web page matches scroll onto the screen, all of them listing the name Dave Corzine in one form or another. After reading through two of them and becoming even more angry at Dave Corzine for not having his own web page, but being notable enough to be a hit *so* many times, I offer a man behind the front desk $20 to compile a fact sheet. Within a half an hour, I find this to be true of Mr. David Corzine:

Born 1956. Attended Hersey High School in Arlington Heights, Illinois, and DePaul University in Chicago. Scored 46 points in single basketball game vs. Louisville in 1976. Drafted by the Washington Bullets in the first round of the NBA Draft in 1978. Played for the Chicago Bulls 1982-1989 and the Seattle Supersonics 1989-1991. Has a red beard and is white and pale.

Current whereabouts: unknown.

I leave the library without paying the librarian his $20—he gets paid to be there already—and decide that even though I could re-catch the El and make it back to work for the last two hours of my shift, I go home.

Dave Corzine, from what I can tell, is a local sports hero. I have not heard of him before and the information found on the Internet does not remind me of hearing of him. On my sixteen-and-a-third-block walk to my one-room apartment, it occurs to me that a lot of the people who are calling my apartment looking for Dave Corzine don't know he doesn't live in my apartment because they don't know Dave Corzine. Dave Corzine is a rich guy who doesn't want to be called by strangers at his real number. While it is remotely possible that Dave Corzine had once been available at my phone number, that my phone number was once indeed Dave Corzine's and the people calling my apartment are merely acting on outdated information, it is much, much more likely that Dave Corzine has given out my number—a random number—*on purpose.*

This is how I see it: Dave Corzine gives out a random (my) number to people *on purpose* because he doesn't want to speak with these people, knowing that they will call the apartment of this random person (me) looking for Dave Corzine (him) and never reach Dave Corzine. While the random person (me) deals with all of the random people Dave Corzine does not want to deal with, Dave Corzine is busy in his mansion drinking highballs and dealing only with the people he wants to, the people to whom he has given his real phone number, Dave Corzine's phone number.

Before formulating this theory, I had not harbored any ill feelings toward Dave Corzine, figuring one honest mistake— as severely damaging to my well-being as it has been—was just that, *one honest mistake*. But all of that has changed. Now that I know the truth, I loathe Dave Corzine like no person can loathe another, and I am filled with just one feeling for the man who has cursed me by sending his unwanted queries my way: hate. Pure and true hate.

Nettendorf is in love with me.

Nettendorf is an average-looking man. He is 5'9". He has black hair and white teeth with no glasses or facial hair. He is not thin or fat. He could be either twenty-five or forty-five. His hands and face tan during the summer and pale in the winter. He will lose his hair when he is older, but has not lost much as of yet. He does not wear cologne, although every other day I can smell aftershave. There are no pictures of his family, friends, or pets on his (our) upholstered wall. He receives no calls and no mail. All of Nettendorf's shirts are solid while his ties are simply patterned: vertical stripes, horizontal stripes, polka dots of all sizes, always matching his solid brown, black, or navy slacks. If he uses the washroom, it is before work, during lunch, or after work. Nettendorf neither farts nor belches, but occasionally he sighs, mostly upon the completion of an encounter with a client, directly followed by a pronounced "Bliss."

Nettendorf is the man who does the exact same thing that I do except at different times. He is the man with whom I work who is in love with me.

He is pathetic.

I know Nettendorf is in love with me because he never looks at me or speaks to me. In our office, we have an average of twenty-eight minutes a day when neither of us is dealing with a customer. I've counted. Nearly half of these twenty-eight minutes are spent with one of us at the 7-Up machine down the hall or me in the bathroom, which, unlike Nettendorf, I use as frequently as I can. The remaining minutes are spent with Nettendorf looking at me behind my back and telling me what he wants me to know by not saying a word.

It is this unprofessed love that makes Nettendorf so pathetic.

Mistake me, however, not: If such a decree came forth, I would not think Nettendorf any more redeeming in any way. If Nettendorf's love were out in the open, he would simply be less pathetic. Under no circumstances, I must tell you, would I require Nettendorf's love, let alone think him anything but merely *somewhat* pathetic.

What makes Nettendorf tolerable—as tolerable, at least, as my job—is that, unlike most people with whom I associate— those who *do* speak to me—Nettendorf never asks me, while at work, if he can speak to Dave Corzine.

For this kindness, he might one day expect me to love him in return. For this assumption, I have no reaction. I simply do not care.

Between Nettendorf's secret admiration and Dave Corzine's cruel torture, I have come to this conclusion: I live in what I call a "bidichotomal existence." On one side, I have the adoring Nettendorf and his inability to express for me what I find both obvious and nauseating, my very existence giving him, silently, a reason to exist himself. On the other side, I live in a one-sided relationship with Dave Corzine: I speak with those people he does not want to speak to but who want to speak to him, while he, in turn, speaks only to those people he wants to speak to. Two dichotomies, two men, with only me in common. Bidichotomal.

Each of these men, Dave Corzine and Nettendorf, are planets reeling me in. I am being pulled by two centers of gravity, each wanting me to collide with their cores. Such treatment would normally pull a body apart, but somehow, some way, through a series of coincidences, similar to and as plentiful as those that led to the creation of the earth sixty billion years ago, the gravitational pulls of Nettendorf and Dave Corzine balance my existence, keep me in tune, keep me from being ripped apart.

Of course, if anything should happen to break this balance between these two heavenly bodies, my two-sun universe, I would be obliterated. No one could predict what exactly would happen, but a small entity like myself could not survive. At best, my universe would cave into itself, erasing my existence in this reality as if sucked into a black hole. A floating cloud of dust and gases. I am not sure if not existing is anything like ceasing to exist, so a change in the balances of Nettendorf and Dave Corzine could, if done by my own hand, be considered suicide. Since I am not going to move my hand in such a direction—and it's not as if I could if I wanted to—this doesn't seem likely.

What would happen if either of these separate entities were altered on their own? Say if calls to Dave Corzine stopped coming to my apartment or if Nettendorf quit his (our) job. What I do know is that I'm not ready to find out. Yet, I am confident that all will remain the same between Nettendorf and me and me and Dave Corzine. It is not as if I care enough to investigate, but I cannot imagine what could possibly happen to break our balances, to knock this planet off its orbit, to ever so possibly go wrong.

The morning after my trip to the library, Nettendorf tells me that Dave Corzine called when I was out, that Dave Corzine will be visiting our office sometime later that day.

Nettendorf continues to talk, about Dave Corzine, I think, but I am not sure, as I cannot hear anything. Like space, our one-room office with its telephone, desk, and counter, has become a vacuum: no sound in, no sound out. Like an astronaut watching his spacewalk cut short by a rip in his spacesuit, I watch Nettendorf's mouth move around his words, his eyes bat open and shut upon me, the edges of his lips crowning upward in a smile. "Dave Corzine," he keeps saying. I can see it: the tip of his tongue smacking off the back of his front teeth to form the "D," his mouth opening wide to pronounce the long "A," and the tips of the same front teeth dipping down to the front of his bottom lip before pulling back into his open mouth, sounding out the "Vuh" sound. "Dave," he says; I cannot watch or describe "Corzine," for I have fainted.

During my faint-sleep, I dream of total strangers calling my house looking for Nettendorf, and a tall, rich, white man with a red beard answering phones at our cubicle desk. It feels like fool's paradise: Everything I see tells me I am in heaven, but that I've entered without invitation. For the first time I can recall, I sweat in my dreams.

A quick note: I do not believe in Heaven. Not in the Biblical sense, anyway, and I do not know enough about the world's other major religions to know whether or not I believe in their Heavens, either. When I used the word "heaven" (lower case H) to describe the place I'm visiting in what I've referred to as my "faint-sleep," I am simply referring to "heaven" in the general sense, what Webster might describe as "... a state or place of complete happiness or rest ..." (*Webster's New World Dictionary* 623). I am not a religious person—in a state of total awareness or out cold—and I do not care if it appears, in my desperate hour, that I have turned to God, gods, or a god.

I meant "heaven" in the general sense.

Just so we're clear.

"Mr. Nettendorf asked me to come down," are the words that wake me from my faint-sleep. I open my eyes and I see a very tall, very white man in a stylish charcoal sport coat, sunglasses roosting in his hair, his head slightly bowed, either to get a closer look at me or to keep from tapping against the rather low drop ceiling. He has a salt-and-pepper red beard. I have never seen this man before and I do not recognize his voice, but without any reservation, I know that it is Dave Corzine. He is looking down at me from above.

"Has he come around?" Nettendorf says. My eyes follow his voice and find him on the phone, which he hangs up. "An ambulance is on the way. They promised less than an hour."

I lift my head off the warm ground and before I can take a breath, I feel my neck give and the back of my head thump against the sculpted carpet.

"Hey," Dave Corzine says. He scoops an enormous hand under my head, the other below my back. Before I can protest or reach out to make our embrace symmetrical, Dave Corzine lifts me up as if I were a feather—space and time hurling with me toward the ceiling like a wormhole—and places me on the counter where I usually deal with in-person complaints half the day.

"There you go," he says. He slides his hands out from under me, letting my head slam against the counter like lead.

Nettendorf appears on the opposite side of the counter as Dave Corzine. The two of them peer down, occasionally looking up at each other. The phone rings without mercy and the fluorescent lights flicker, sending tics down my shoulders and inner thighs.

"Do you want me to wait with you?" Dave Corzine says to Nettendorf.

"Wait with me for what?"

"The ambulance," answers Dave Corzine. He looks at his watch, down at me, then back at his watch.

"That's OK," Nettendorf says. "It could be an hour."

Nettendorf and Dave Corzine disappear from my line of vision, leaving me in the company of the phone and fluorescent lighting fixtures. I can hear Nettendorf talking in the background, near my feet, and Dave Corzine, his voice deeper and more confident than Nettendorf's, saying "Yes" approximately every sixteen seconds. This goes on for approximately four minutes and twelve seconds, which, very uncoincidentally, is the average time an encounter with a client takes on a normal working day.

Dave Corzine has come in to collect on a no-good electronic good.

Nettendorf goes into his practiced speech about how to call *this* number and wait *this many* days for the refund and how to take his refund to *this* store—one that happens to sell our warranties—to find the best replacement for his retired good.

("Retired" is how Nettendorf and I refer to the items our company's clients have bought warranties on and have broken.)

Dave Corzine says "Yes" to all three of Nettendorf's instructions. I feel the sound and air quality of the room change as Dave Corzine and Nettendorf shake hands, and then again as Dave Corzine leaves, leaves our office, the office where he had just been—where he had just been with me. Nettendorf's pen sounds like a jet engine as he scribbles it across Dave Corzine's claim form, the plane crashing into the mountain as Nettendorf signs his elaborate, cowardly signature. A drawer in the file cabinet under the counter opens, some file folders are shuffled back and forth, then the file cabinet door closes like the lid of a coffin.

"Are you still with us?" Nettendorf says to me, reappearing in my crosshairs, blocking out some of the fluorescent streams that are reaching down to grab me and pull me into the drop ceiling.

I turn my head toward him. Nettendorf is beautiful.

"That was Dave Corzine, you know. *The* Dave Corzine. Right here, in *our* office."

I look back at the reaching light, wanting Nettendorf to move so that all the rays can work together to lift me up into its heavens.

"I need to call him," I say to Nettendorf.

"Call him?" Nettendorf looks down at me. He is like a surgeon, the way he's staring at me.

"I need to call Dave Corzine." I have conviction in my voice, but add, "When I get home tonight."

Nettendorf stops staring at me and disappears from the light. I feel the file cabinet drawer open again, the file folders shuffle.

"Here's his claim form," Nettendorf says, holding it out to me, to my peripheral vision.

I cannot move. I instruct: "Hold it in front of my eyes."

I stare up at the complaint form and work to focus. Light is burned onto my retinas. Nettendorf's fingers come into focus first, the words and numbers on the claim form following. I scan the form until I reach the "HOME PHONE NUMBER" line and read the number.

"Maybe you could set me up with some Bulls tickets."

I cannot go home and call and ask for Dave Corzine at the number hanging above my eyes. If I did, I would only get a busy signal.

"Bliss," Nettendorf says. "That would be bliss."

# Green

Instead of a vacation, my husband invites my old lovers over for two weeks, just to clear the air, he says, and change the pace. I'd had no idea the pace needed changing, or that he'd known about half my affairs. The guest list, though, proved complete, every man who made it past second base, some names I didn't even recognize. ("Larry Benson?" I asked. "A.K.A. 'Clint Hood.' Sigma Kappa party, sophomore year," he explained.) My heart had been set on Paris, but it *was* my husband's year to choose. Last summer's trek through the Andes had been my third pick in a row, so really, I had one hand tied behind my back.

To my surprise, all the RSVPs came back affirmative. All of them. No one declined—no conflicts, no prior commitments, no regrets. No one had died, though some had questions: *Do I bring my own towel? Where are you registered? Can I request vegan meals?* We rented a shuttle for four airport runs, warned the neighbors about extra cars on the street. Sleeping arrangements would be difficult, even with the girls at my dad's, but we'd make it work. I would, anyway, if I was to ever see the Louvre.

Everyone looked thinner, was my first impression, and richer than I would have guessed. Some I did not recognize, not until they'd slapped on their name tags, and even then, it was hazy. After all, I'd known several—at least a dozen—less than a night. That dozen seemed most cordial, though, pecking my cheek, complimenting my house, my dress, reinvoking, I realized later, magic that had already proven effective. I spied my husband during these encounters, mixing drinks and shaking hands, and wondered if one of his eyes remained fixed on the stairs leading to the bedroom.

The longer affairs, the steadies and ex-fiancés, were, at best, awkward, and, at worst, confrontational. For every apology, I received five questions as to *Why?* then, worse, not very subtle inquiries as to my current happiness. One offer, flat out: *Why don't you and I get out of here?* "It would be a long two weeks for everyone else if I did," I answered, and after he walked away, I realized I'd not exactly said no.

My lovers calmed over the next week, everyone's curiosity quenched, as the idea I wasn't sleeping with any of them again firmly planted itself. What struck me as odd was how much like my husband all these men were, or at least became. They picked up his habits, his pattern of speech, even his scent. They ate what he ate and told the same jokes. Each and every one of them made it known, eventually, how surprised he was there wasn't at least one woman in the mix, followed by either a wink or a *Yeah, I wish,* to which I replied, "I'll bet you do." Still, I found a comfort in this sameness, better than awkwardness or the *Whys?*, an inventory I'd been meaning to sort out, anyway. I enjoyed the two weeks the way someone enjoys mowing the lawn or washing the dishes, a familiarity in routine added to a sense of accomplishment. The perfect future anniversary gift to my husband, I was thinking, until I remembered I had been his first, and as far I knew, his last.

At the end of the vacation, I was sad to see my lovers leave, but knew their newfound affinity with my husband would sustain me in their absence. I wished them the best of luck, encouraging them to never contact us again, reminding them of how unnecessary that would be. My husband echoed this sentiment, thanked them for a wonderful two weeks, and reminded them that the pictures would be up on the Internet soon. Most were pleasant, agreeing to our terms, a tidier ending than any shrink could have milked from me in a thousand sessions.

One of my lovers stayed behind after the others had left. He was the man with the dark hair and green eyes, the one I'd never been able to place. My husband didn't know him, either, even though his name was on the list. He wouldn't ask him to leave. Neither could I. The man remained in our house thereafter, not interfering with our day-to-day lives, but in our house just the same. We would never see him when we looked, but sometimes he'd just be there, sitting next to me on the loveseat, trailing behind on the walk. In our bedroom while we made love. The man never spoke to us or ever asked for anything. But when he appeared, I felt a pain run through me, a pain I could not explain to my husband, not a pain a good husband could understand. Neither could I. Over the years, I would get used to the pain, even start to like it, but it was at these times I couldn't see the man, even remember his face. Or the color of his eyes.

# The Summer Without Grown-Ups

The summer between my graduating from grade school and starting high school, my grandmother turned into a golden bird. I discovered this one day after baseball practice when I rode my bike to her house and found Grandma the canary sitting atop the light fixture in the dining room. For a brief second, our eyes met, and she let out a quiet *tweet*, then launched herself in my direction. Just learning to fly, she struggled her way over to my shoulder, where she dug in with her tiny claws and used her beak to peck at the silver stud in the center of my earlobe.

That's how I knew the yellow bird was my grandmother, her outward hatred of my earring. Earrings were for girls and ex-sailors, she'd said, but it wasn't like I was the first kid to break that barrier. Pat Harkey had his ear pierced first, and the fact he was the best kid on our team seemed like no coincidence. Mike Orie had one the day after Pat, and then the Cline twins, Scott and Gary, each showed up with theirs at our Friday scrimmage with Bol-Mor Lanes. That night I rode to the mall and got my left ear pierced.

I couldn't verify this for sure, but I was already the last guy to get his pubes—thirteen and not a strand to be seen—and one such atrocity was enough. The fear of falling behind weighed down on me like a 100 mph fastball. Sure enough, the next Monday at practice, every single one of us twisted away at our little studs, working that hole, just like the girls with the frosted bangs at the mall had told us to. Our coach didn't like it much—he was a real hard-on—and made us run till the three fat kids on the team puked, yelling that we could stop only to fix our makeup or put in a tampon.

I was taking a lot of shit on all fronts for the earring and thought about taking it out—until I ran into Deirdre and Kendra on the way home from that all-running practice. Deirdre said it was cool—boss, even—and that made up for everyone else. She poked at it with her fingertip and said when the starter took, she'd give me a diamond stud because she'd lost the other and girls had to wear pairs. She said I would look hot in a diamond stud, and that was that.

This was the first time a girl ever touched me on purpose, save some nuns at school, who had routinely kicked the crap out of me for nine years, the last walloping for the earring just that afternoon. Long story short, whatever Coach Hardass, the evil nuns, my grandmother, or my grandmother-the-bird said, I didn't care. Deirdre's little poke was the single greatest moment of my life. The earring stayed.

That was also the summer that Mom left us and Dad turned into a basket case, falling off the planet for over three months. Before all this, I'd promised I would look after Grandma, my last living grandparent, whom Dad said I should treasure. I did my best to stop by after school, dust her baseboards, weed the cracks in her sidewalk, and when it got warm, stroll with her around the block and help her make fun of the neighbors' aluminum siding. Once Mom split for Reno and Dad checked out, I kept my promise, even though Dad would never know, him not deciphering between night and day, let alone knowing the whereabouts of his only offspring. The funny thing was Grandma wasn't Dad's mom—she was Mom's—but Mom was dealing blackjack and living with her former gynecologist. Dad was just being good people because Grandma had always been good to him. The pre-canary Grandma stuff was easy—she was always good for a few bucks, no matter what I did—but once she changed into a bird, I wish I could have asked my dad what the hell I was supposed to do.

The problem was, Dad just didn't care anymore. Right after Mom left, he was in decent spirits, would joke around about her deserting us in a way I'd never heard him talk before: "That OB-GYN, I have to give it to him. He really knows his way around a vagina." It was funny, even though I didn't know what it meant, because Dad laughed and was talking to me in a way I wasn't used to. I was a man. We were a team. I half expected him to give me a beer.

Within a couple of weeks, all the pictures of Mom had the eyes cut out and Dad stopped going to work. Grandma helped with the bills—she had money and she felt guilty about Mom being a deadbeat slut—but once Grandma turned into a canary, it wasn't like she could write checks.

Enter the summer of '88, my summer without grown-ups.

The first week or so of my independence, I didn't see the downside to anything. I got to do what I wanted, when I wanted. I don't think I went to bed before 1 a.m. any of those days. But soon, I thought about the bills, Dad's job, and the dwindling food supply. On top of that, Grandma's property became infested with cats, cats with one thing on their minds: eating Grandma. They littered her front lawn, her front porch, the tire swing in the oak, the *Gary Hart for President* sign, and all the windowsills, too. Once when I was leaving, Grandma tried to fly out the door, but when she spied the cats, scrawny and lurking, she turned ninety degrees, perching herself on a drape rod and not coming down for two days.

The cats reminded me of all of Grandma's boyfriends, from when she was still a woman, a different guy at her house every time we visited, sometimes other guys coming by when a guy was already there. That made my dad grumble, prompting comparisons to his folks. Those grandparents died three weeks apart, Grandpa, as Dad told it, unable to survive without my other grandma. When Mom's dad died, however, Mom's mom started dating right away, maybe a month later at most. She met guys at church, at the mall, the library, some at bars. Mom had been OK with this—which made sense later—but Dad thought it was bad form, that Grandma was some sort of hoochie. Mom would always laugh and tell him he had full license to screw his brains out if she died, that she'd be dead and wouldn't care. He could play the grieving widower card, she suggested, sleep with one of her girlfriends after the funeral, Claire, for example. Claire was the enormous-breasted redhead whose tits I couldn't stop staring at even when I knew she knew I was staring. Dad didn't care for Mom's suggestion, and when Mom left for Nevada, he stood by his word. Claire, to tempt him further, came over a lot, bringing casseroles and things she made in a Crock-Pot, always wearing tank tops, and once, this see-through tube top, the elastic inside stretched to the point of snapping. Once Dad wasn't able to leave the house, let alone have a conversation, Claire's visits stopped. I had been dreaming of her living with us, her showering a lot and getting dressed in Dad's room, maybe forgetting to close the door. In my estimation, that was Dad's biggest mistake, or, as I liked to joke, his two biggest mistakes.

After her earring poke, I thought of Deirdre that summer more than I thought of Claire. Deirdre was a Claire-in-the-making, her bra the only one in our eighth grade class that looked warranted. Plus, Deirdre had touched me voluntarily, promising the diamond stud, and best of all, becoming a groupie for Wells Funeral Home, my Babe Ruth team. Deirdre, her acid-washed jeans, her IOU sweatshirts, and her Claire starter-tits came to every game. Between innings, she and Kendra leaned against the chainlink fence next to our dugout, greeting us when we came in from the field, chatting us up when we were on deck. I took my swings with the fungo and tried to concentrate, to keep my head down on the ball, but I was distracted. At bat, I could hear Deirdre cheer my name, clap when I took a ball, boo the ump if he called a strike. If I got a hit, she'd go apeshit, and with eyes in back of my head, I saw her girls bouncing like gangbusters.

I wished my dad would have made some games—he'd coached me in Little League all five years and was supposed to help out with this team—but the Mom incident knocked him out of the loop. Deirdre more than made up for it, that stunning enthusiasm for mediocrity, her growing appreciation for me. Our team went 3-14 that summer, and for the first time ever, I didn't make the traveling all-star roster. Dad, before he went nuts, used to say you knew a girl loved you when she stuck by you in the bad times. This told me two things: 1) My mom didn't really love my dad, and 2) Deirdre must have had it bad for yours truly.

At mid-July, baseball season ended, and on the home front, supplies ran thin. The mail started to fill with second and final notices. I thought we'd had plenty of food after I used the cash from Grandma's purse to fill up on cereal, canned goods, and frozen stuff for the freezer in the basement, but before long, that stash was history. Somehow, when I wasn't around, Dad managed to eat a bit and go to the bathroom, but even though I'd talked to him, screamed in his face, went so far as to grab him by the shoulders and shake him, he couldn't look me in the eye, give me a single-word response. He just stared off at the ceiling, turned to Jell-O in my hands. I wasn't sure how long we could go on like that. He'd been fired from his job in May and he seemed to be OK with a teenage son having the run of the town. The word FORECLOSURE was playing a prominent role on those letters and on our answering machine. I pictured men from the bank coming in, moving all our stuff to the lawn, leaving Dad and the bed for last, finally pushing him into the driveway. I wondered what he'd do then, if he'd just stare at the sky, not even realize what had happened. Worse, somebody would figure out that a kid was living without a competent guardian. After locking Dad up in the loony bin, they'd call Mom, not get an answer, take me to Grandma's, find out she was a bird, then ship me off to foster care. There some super-Christian freaks with ten other kids would make me say rosaries in the nude while they shot Super 8s.

By that point, I'd gotten used to being able to do whatever I wanted. This was a fact I didn't take advantage of early in the summer, concentrating on baseball, playing video games, and my daily pube watch, a chart of my (non-) progress on the calendar above the trash can. Every day I'd wake up, hoping to have a short, curly hair in the middle of my abdomen, but every morning I'd mark an "N" and move on. Some days I'd work at it, rubbing Dad's aftershave down there, as from what I understood, that's how he got the hair on his face to come back the next day. I'd also think sexy thoughts, of Claire and Deirdre mostly, sometimes both of them together, showing each other their breasts, washing each other's hair, scooping ice cream into bowls and licking each others' scoopers. Neither the Old Spice nor the dirty daydreams did me any good. Every morning, I was as hairless as the day I was born.

The real problem was, at the high school in my district, your first eight weeks in gym consisted of swimming, which meant getting naked in the locker room every day. I was soon dreading the seniors, them seeing my smooth bod and telling every girl in our school, every girl at the Catholic school, their moms and sisters, their aunts and grandmas, every woman they'd ever meet again, forever, until they died. I still had five weeks until school started, but I was guessing that when your body started pube production, you didn't turn into Tom Selleck overnight—it would take a while for the full complement to manifest. Procuring a normal, hairy physique was looking impossible. With all that had gone wrong, I was hoping for at least this one miracle.

That miracle, I thought, came in the form of Cunny. Cunny—a.k.a. Drew Cunningham—was my best friend since kindergarten, but the summer before, he moved to Florida with his mom. Like my mom, Cunny's dad had an affair and skipped town, but instead of turning into a throw pillow like my dad did, Cunny's mom moved back with her parents in St. Petersburg and got her real estate license. Within six months, they had their own place and Cunny was living on the beach, making new friends, not caring if his dad was dead or alive.

One night right after baseball season ended, Cunny called to say his mom had some seminar in San Diego and he wondered if he could stay with me for the week. His mom was going to stick him on a plane, then *voilà*, a whole week with my best pal. The fact I had the house to myself just made things more perfect. I was afraid Cunny's mom was going to want to talk to my dad, or my mom—since I never told Cunny about Mom leaving—but Cunny floored me: His mom didn't want to talk to anyone. She just took our words for it, two thirteen-year-old boys, and bought him the ticket. Things were turning around, and it couldn't have come at a better time.

That Sunday, I rode my bike to the airport, seven miles one way, found the terminal for Cunny's plane, and met him at his gate. As he walked down the tunnel toward me, I noticed he looked different, taller, tanner, and way older than me. His hair was blonder and longer, too, and with his mirror sunglasses, he looked like a *Miami Vice* henchman. On our way out to my bike, I explained how I'd gotten there and how we were going to have to ride all the way with him on the handlebars, that it took me over two hours by myself. Cunny just about beat me up. He had two big suitcases with him, plus his school bag, and we'd never make it, not if we took all week. We sat down at the airport Burger King and I told him the whole story, which I hated to do, embarrassed about my mom, about not telling him. Cunny had been there. His dad had run off—with his mom's sister, to boot—so he knew pain. Aside from moving away, he had to go to a counselor every week, an old guy in sandals who asked him about his dreams and how often he touched himself. Cunny was tough, though. He was kinda mad I never told him about my mom, but it was cool once I filled him in about my dad and how we'd have the place to ourselves. After a major think session, we used some of the money Cunny's mom gave him, two hundred dollars, to hail a cab. I left my bike chained to a stop sign outside, figuring I could just ride it home a week later, when another cab dropped Cunny back off.

Cunny tried talking to my dad when we got home, and for a second, I thought Dad might snap out of it. When Dad wouldn't answer his questions, Cunny waved his arms in front of Dad's face. When Dad wouldn't blink, Cunny poked Dad in the chest. When Dad didn't flinch, Cunny gave him a kiss on the forehead. Eventually, Cunny, determined, showed Dad his butt, cut one of Dad's credit cards in half, and at last breath, peed in Dad's bed, on the comforter, on the sheets, and across

Dad's pillows. I was sure Dad would wake up and kill Cunny, whom he never really liked, but Dad still wouldn't move.

"Wow," Cunny said, and we gave up.

We dipped into Cunny's money again to order a pizza. We played video games and ate, talking about each other's fucked-up dads. Cunny didn't really like talking about his anymore, still mad about the aunt thing, so we spent a lot of time on mine, what we were going to do. I told Cunny about the mortgage, how any day, the bank could show up with the cops and a moving van. I asked Cunny if his mom could help and he said no, that she just sold houses. Bankers, he said, were the meanest assholes on Earth because they wanted their money no matter what. He also pointed out that if we told his mom, she would call the state and I'd be in that foster home by the end of the day. His mom was a real adult, he said, the only one between our four parents, and there was no bargaining with real adults.

"What about that rich grandma of yours?" Cunny said later, us falling asleep in my room. "Can't you live with her?"

I wanted to tell him about Grandma changing into a canary, how she was in her huge house across town, singing her songs and eating stale white bread that I crumbled on the counter. But Cunny wouldn't believe me, as good of a friend as he was. He'd have to see it for himself.

"I'll take you to see her tomorrow," I said.

I knew Cunny was thinking she was dead, that we'd go to her house and I'd have my grandmother in a bathtub, just rotting away in a pretty dress. But he just went to bed, said, "OK." Cunny was cool that way, took what I said for what it was worth and left the rest alone. Cunny, really, was more of an adult than any of our parents. What kind of mom puts her kid on a plane without talking to another adult on the other end? Cunny was going to get me out of this if anyone was. I fell asleep, him on my floor next to my bed, and I felt confident for the first time that things might work out.

The next day, instead of helping me save my Dad and my house, Cunny got a hand job from Deirdre. On our way to Grandma's that morning, we ran into Deirdre and Kendra on their way to the mall to get their nails done. I never had the stones, not that whole summer, to invite Deirdre over to the house, and right there it hit me, what was I waiting for? Deirdre and Kendra and Chrissy Stamos and Jenna Kalinski and Julie Perkey could have all come to my house for a raucous sex party and Dad wouldn't have moved an inch. Cunny was in the presence of girls for all of ten seconds before he was offering my place up as a private chateau. He still had a hundred and eighty dollars to spend, which he pulled out and showed the ladies, explaining that my parents were gone on vacation in San Diego, that they'd asked him personally to come up from Florida and look after me. Deirdre and Kendra had always been, in general, indifferent to Cunny. They might not have remembered he left. Now that Cunny was back in town, older and leaner and most assuredly in possession of a major spread of pubes, they were all about going to my house. Worse, neither girl looked at me the entire way, their eyes fixed on tall, tan, blond Cunny. I began to wonder if girls could sense if a guy had his pubes or not. I was terrified.

At my house, I ran ahead to my Dad's room and shut the door, and that's all it took to take care of that problem. It was kind of sad, I thought, treating Dad like that, but I'd worry about that later, the girl of my fantasies willingly in my lair. Cunny turned on the TV, *The Price Is Right*, which was the only thing we could agree on watching, the rest either soap operas or lamer game shows. Deirdre and Kendra sat on my couch, one on either side of Cunny, and when I came back with four glasses of orange pop, I had to sit on the easy chair on the other side of the room. Cunny made fun of all the ecstatic losers jumping up and down. Deirdre and Kendra thought he was hilarious, no matter what he said. After the Showcase Showdown, the girls went to the bathroom together. While they were gone, Cunny told me they were lezzing it up, that they couldn't stand to *not* lez it up for more than an hour at a time. He dared me to go and put my ear next to the door so I could hear them lezzing it up, but I wouldn't, saying I didn't want to hear girls pissing. Right as they came out, Cunny said, "Why not?"

Deirdre and Kendra emerged and said that they had to go, that Kendra was supposed to be home at one to go with her family to Service Merchandise. Her dad was taking off early from work so they could buy a new TV. Cunny said that was cool, and when he glanced at my TV, I knew what he was thinking. But Cunny didn't say anything, instead pointing out to Deirdre that *she* didn't have to go just because Kendra did, asking if they ever went anywhere without each other. Deirdre said that it would indeed be cool to stay and party at my house, all the game shows and Nehi she could handle, I guess. Kendra said that she didn't mind. Cunny suggested I walk Kendra out, or heck, all the way home, all kinds of baddies roaming the street, just waiting for the inseparable pair to split up so they could descend.

I wanted to leave Cunny in my house with Deirdre as much as I'd wanted Deirdre to know about my pubeless jock scalp. Then I remembered that Kendra lived just a couple of blocks away from my Grandma, and since I'd spent all day at the airport the day before, I didn't check in on her. That had been the first day all summer I didn't stop by. I wanted to make sure she had bread and water, that no cats had found a secret way in, that she wasn't lonely without me. I would never forgive myself if my Grandma the canary died on my watch. I agreed to walk Kendra home, thinking I'd run into Grandma's, stay five minutes, then be back, all within an hour.

On the way to her house, Kendra freaked the shit out of me when she said Deirdre liked Cunny, that I was a good friend for letting them "have" my place. Kendra asked if I would come to her house at seven and walk her back, how her family would be back from TV shopping by then and done with dinner. It seemed like a tall order, me suddenly in charge of transporting Kendra, but I couldn't say no. Somehow I knew Cunny wouldn't let me, plus, if it somehow made Deirdre happy, I was still willing. The rest of the way, Kendra and I walked in near silence. Once I asked her what classes she'd signed up for and we found out we were in biology together. I told her that it would be cool, that maybe we'd be lab partners, but really, it wasn't that cool. She agreed that it was cool, though I'm pretty sure she was as indifferent about it as I was. In front of her house I told her I hoped she got a cool TV, and if her dad was cool, he'd flip for a remote. Again she agreed that it would be cool, and even though we seemed to agree a lot on what was cool, I was glad to be rid of her.

When I unlocked the door to Grandma's, another bird flew out of the house, right past my head, into the oak out front. I didn't know what kind of bird it was, maybe a sparrow, but I couldn't be sure. I called out for Grandma, which on most days would bring her to me, singing and drilling at my earring. At first, Grandma didn't fly out and I thought the worst, tiny yellow Grandma lifeless on the floor. At second call she came, gliding in from the kitchen. Maybe she was mad because I skipped a day, or maybe the other bird freaked her out. Either way, Grandma the canary was all right, no tragic death on my conscience, her song making me forget, just for a few minutes, about Deirdre and Cunny, my mom, my dad, and my persistent lack of pubes.

When I got back home, I expected to see Cunny and Deirdre sitting close on the sofa, maybe even kissing, all over each other like lovers on soap operas. They weren't anywhere I could see, not answering when I called. I checked on my dad, who appeared to be fine, and I figured they'd gone out. Cunny had that $180 in his pocket, so they most likely walked downtown for something to eat. I pictured Cunny saying, "Order anything you want," pulling the hundred and four twenties out of his jeans. All we had left in the house was canned soup and about a dozen pot pies in the freezer downstairs. It's not like Cunny was going to break out some Chicken and Stars or throw a Hungry-Man in the microwave if Deirdre got peckish. We didn't even have any chips.

With Cunny and Deirdre gone, I went to the basement to get a turkey pie. On my way up the stairs, I heard giggling coming from the laundry room and figured Cunny was hiding, ready to jump out and scare the shit out of me. At first I didn't see anything except the washer, dryer, and mountain of clothes I didn't know how to wash. In the back corner was a little room with just a toilet and sink, and under the plywood door, I could see the light on and shadows moving around. I thought about going in, surprising Cunny before he could jump out, but then I froze: What if he was taking a crap? I didn't want to see that, my best friend shitting, his parts covered in wild, bushy hair. That would make for a strange week.

Then Cunny came out of the bathroom on his own— with Deirdre. They were smiling and holding hands and Cunny had this look on his face like he just discovered a planet. Both of them said, "Hey," then we stood there, in the laundry room, staring at each other, the pot pie defrosting in my hand. Deirdre broke the silence by saying she had to go, that she would be back later with Kendra. We could play a board game or they could watch me and Cunny play video games. We let her go up and let herself out, but Cunny yelled, "See you tonight!" before the door slammed shut.

When he was sure she was gone, Cunny made the internationally accepted gesture for jerking off, shaking his fist in front of him like he was plunging a toilet. He was grinning and nodding, too, and I knew he was referring to Deirdre. We'd been saying "jerk-off" for years, a million times over, calling kids "jerk-offs," occasionally changing it to "jack-off." Once, when I was late for practice, Pat Harkey yelled out, the whole team already running sprints, that I was "... probably jerking off." But now, this was different, and I knew, from the way Deirdre ran off, that it was good. And that it was supposed to be me instead of him.

Cunny was kind of mad that I didn't want him to talk about it, that I didn't want the details. At one point, when he said he couldn't figure out the hooks on Deirdre's bra, the thought of that bra and what was inside piqued my imagination. But when he mimicked grabbing them and salivated over how soft they were, I told him I didn't want the gory details. We just hung out the rest of the day and played Nintendo, Cunny kicking my ass at most every game.

At 7:30 on the nose, Deirdre and Kendra tapped on the screen door and Cunny jumped up to let them in. We watched TV, me in the chair across the room, Kendra on the couch, Cunny and Deirdre arm in arm on the floor. Once in a while, I'd see them holding hands, and a few times, Cunny ran his fingers down her arm. Deirdre liked it, that much was obvious. After all, they'd been involved in a jerk-off in my basement— why wouldn't she like him touching her arm with his fingertips?

At 10:30 we watched *The Tonight Show*, even though it was Joan Rivers, and as soon as the monologue was over, Kendra announced she had to go. Like it was his house, like he was my dad, Cunny told me to walk Kendra home again, even waving his finger toward the outside, pointing me in the right direction. Kendra wanted Deirdre to go with her, but Cunny said he'd walk Deirdre home and I should stick with Kendra. When I asked why Cunny and Deirdre weren't leaving with me and Kendra, Cunny said he had to go to the bathroom and they'd leave right after. Kendra started whining about missing curfew, so I relented. Again, Cunny had my house, and everything else that was mine, to himself.

That's how things pretty much went the rest of the week. Little by little, Cunny and Deirdre got bolder. On Tuesday, when I got back from walking Kendra home, Deirdre was gone and Cunny announced they were dating, going steady, that he was going to leave his sky blue Members Only jacket for her to wear to school in the fall. On Wednesday, Deirdre and Cunny held hands the whole day, and while we watched TV, they made out, right in front of us, on the living room floor. Kendra started asking me questions, mostly about where my parents were and why I liked soup and pot pies so much. I told her that I just did, that they were my favorite.

That night in my room, Cunny surprised me by saying he didn't want to spend the rest of the trip with Deirdre, that we'd hang out all day Thursday. We would play ball in the park and spend some of his mom's money at the arcade. He even proposed buying a new Nintendo game, *Double Dragon*, which I'd salivated over but couldn't afford. Cunny still had over $100, and since it was already going to be the weekend, he'd cover the bill. I was his best friend and he didn't fly up here to spend it with a girl.

The next morning, we played catch out on my front lawn, just as Cunny had promised. As soon as Deirdre and Kendra turned the corner onto my block, however, we were done. Cunny was all like, "You and Kendra should just split for a while, man. How about four or five hours?" He even waved a ten in my face, told me to hang out somewhere, wait for the matinees to start and see a movie. On him. What pissed me off the most was how he made a crack about pot pies, saying I could get two dozen with a ten dollar bill, that Kendra would help me carry them home. I wanted to punch him in the lip, but Kendra touched my arm and said that we had to talk, that we should take a walk and leave the lovebirds alone. Kendra sounded serious—no girl had ever had to have a talk with me before—and I wondered if she knew about all the jerking off that was going on in my basement. I had a feeling she did, because girls talked to each other more than boys did, my dad once told me. They only kept secrets from us.

Kendra and I walked the opposite direction of her house because she said she was bored with that direction. We didn't talk at first and I had a strong feeling she hated me, blamed me and my empty house for Deirdre ditching her. In third grade, our desks were next to each almost half the year and I'd even had a crush on her for a while. It started the day she bent over to pick up her pencil and her Brownie uniform lifted, exposing her mint green underwear. The infatuation ended a month later when Sister Evangelista Marie moved the class' desks around, the length of the room too much to sustain my affections.

Now we were together again, and Kendra knew about the jerking off, I ascertained, so I said to her, "Yeah, they're like jerking off every single day!" Then I added, because Kendra seemed into it, "That kid really knows his way around a vagina."

Kendra laughed and made the jerk-off motion with her fist, only next to her mouth, pushing her tongue into the side of her cheek. I knew as a fact Cunny and Deirdre were making out—putting their tongues in each other's cheeks—so I assumed Kendra meant they made out during the jerking off. That made sense to me, so I nodded and did the jerk-off motion while putting my tongue in my cheek, too. Kendra said I looked like I was good at that and I took it as a compliment.

At the mall, we tried to go see *Coming to America*, but the guy with the bowtie in the booth wouldn't sell us tickets, saying the movie was R-rated and they were cracking down. We used $4.50 of Cunny's money to see *Who Framed Roger Rabbit* instead. Kendra had seen it already, so she knew all about what happened and ruined every scene, including the ending, me not wanting to know things I was supposed to know later. After the movie, we thought it would be safe to go back to my house, that Cunny and Deirdre would be done simultaneously making out and jerking off. On the way, we passed a lot of places to get food—the smell of the potato cakes from the Arby's almost killed me—but I didn't have enough money left for both of us and knew enough manners than to buy just for me. We just walked back to my house, gone over three hours, and I hoped Cunny would make good on his promise to hang out, that Deirdre and Kendra would just go away.

A block away from my place, Deirdre came running up to us and told me that I had to go home, telling Kendra they had to go and go now. I told Deirdre that I could do whatever I wanted because it was my house, that she should stop telling me what to do. I added a few "fucks" in there to let her know I meant business. I was souring on Deirdre since that morning, she and Cunny a new team, and honestly, I thought Kendra was cooler even though she didn't have a diamond stud for me, let alone the tits. Kendra was just cooler, and I wondered if that meant something. My dad liked my mom more than Claire, and Claire was the epitome of sexy, her big breasts and red hair and provocative little shirts. Yet my dad was comatose in his bed, his beard surrounding his neck, and our lives going to hell, all because he seemed to really like my mom and not heavenly Claire. Maybe my mom was cool in the way Kendra was cool. Or at least she used to be, because my mom was a whole lot more like Deirdre at that point, doing things with the wrong guy. After me telling her off, Deirdre just gave Kendra that look, like it was time to go, and off they want, Deirdre wishing me luck as she rushed off. For some reason, I think she meant it.

When I got inside my house, my heart jumped over a beat because my dad was on the phone in the kitchen, standing there in his bathrobe and T-shirt and underwear, Cunny slumped quiet at the kitchen table. You could tell Cunny had been crying, his eyes with those tiny bloodshot lines and puffy lids, but he bucked up when he saw me, wiping his face with his shirttail and sitting up straight in the chair. My dad was staring, too, at the calendar on the fridge, my Ns leading up to that morning. When he saw me come in, he hung up the phone and asked me, straight off: "Kevin, what day is it?" My dad really didn't know the date, and when I hesitated in telling him, he said, "Three months?" like he was going to cry, too.

Dad pointed to the table and I sat down across from Cunny. I wanted my friend to tell me what happened, tell me why he was crying, but my dad updated me before I could ask.

"Cunny here—who I thought lived in Florida—was having sex with a girl on my bed," Dad said. "Right next to me."

I looked at Cunny, who was still looking down but trying to hide a smirk. After all that had happened, all that was going to happen, Cunny thought this was funny. If I had the guts, I would have jumped across the table and punched Cunny in the eye. I hated him.

Because everything happened at his house, with him home, Dad couldn't exactly call Mrs. Cunningham—now Ms. Grace—and tell her the whole story. He and Cunny made a silent agreement: Dad wouldn't tell Cunny's mom that he'd been having sex in his house all week and Cunny wouldn't tell his mom that my dad *let* him have sex in his house all week. In the end, Cunny maybe did seem like the true adult, having sex, traveling around the country, lying to cover his own ass.

❧

The next few days, Cunny and I watched a lot more TV, played more Nintendo, and ate more pizza, my dad busy putting his life back together. He had a savings account I didn't know about, and for the most part, we were able to catch up on all our bills, including the mortgage. It wiped us out, but we'd be OK, he insisted. Dad didn't get his old job back, which sucked, eighteen years with the company, but they set him up with a few contacts, and on Monday, he was going on an interview. It would be for less money and he'd have to start his retirement package from scratch, but really, it could have been worse.

On Sunday, my dad drove us to the airport to drop off Cunny. Cunny apologized to my dad at the gate and my dad accepted, shaking his hand, then Cunny hugged me, told me he'd call when he got home. As soon as Cunny was out of sight, Dad told me that Cunny wasn't allowed to visit anymore, but I already knew I'd never see Cunny again, probably never talk to him, either.

Halfway home, I realized my bike was still at the airport so my dad turned around to go and get it. When I found the sign I thought I'd left it chained to, my bike wasn't there. Instead of going inside to ask someone, my dad drove to Sportmart and bought me a new bike. My old bike was an orange Schwinn Predator, but Dad insisted I get a ten-speed, saying I was too old for dirt bikes. I picked one out that was maroon with charcoal gray trim. When I asked him why he was buying me a new bike—I thought I'd be grounded or sent off to military school—Dad said he was sorry about what happened and that was that.

The next day, my dad at his interview and me three days removed from my last visit, I rode my new bike to Grandma's.

I got really scared really quick when I got close because all the cats were gone, every single one, as if there were no reason to try and get inside anymore. My grandma could just be gone and I'd never see her again. Like Cunny. Like my mom. Things came in threes, I'd heard, so I was half-expecting it to be true.

As soon as I got the door open, my grandmother flew up to me, doing loop-de-loops around my head, bobbing up and down, zigzagging in every direction. At first I thought Grandma didn't recognize me, or just the opposite, she did recognize me and was angry. I pictured her being out of bread at that point—I'd brought some for her in my backpack—maybe even out of water, though I'd left the toilet open just in case of emergencies. My grandma wasn't mad at all, it turned out. She was trying to get my attention, get me to follow her. She kept flying into her bedroom and singing, luring me in her direction. I wasn't sure what I'd find, but if Grandma wanted to show me something, I knew it had to be important.

On the dresser across from her bed, Grandma had built a nest out of torn scraps of the drapes, placemats, and dish towels. I thought the nest looked damn impressive, her first I assumed, but when I looked closer, I was even more thrilled. Inside the nest lay three blue, speckled eggs, my grandma's eggs, what I could only assume were the product of Grandma and that bird who had flown out the door that one day. My grandma was going to be a mom again, which I thought was impossible because of her change of life, so the eggs had to be a miracle. It was a happy occasion, but I couldn't help but think that other bird was another deadbeat parent, a runaway dad, probably out jerking off with some other girl bird in another city. But if my dad could raise me by himself—I believed with my whole heart he was back on track—I knew Grandma could raise three birds without anyone, that she would do a fantastic job.

In case Grandma wanted to fortify her nest, I placed some gauze from the medicine cabinet on the dresser, slicing strips off with a steak knife, pieces she could manage with her beak. I set a piece of white bread there, too, and refilled the coffee cup with cool water. I spent almost a half an hour in my grandma's room, sitting on her bed, watching her eat and reinforce her nest, and listened to her sing, the song as pretty as any she had sung. I made a plan for the next morning to dig some worms from our garden and ride them over. Better yet, I'd ride over and dig the worms out of Grandma's garden so they'd be fresher and juicier, still squirming, still alive. Maybe I'd ride to the library and look up books on birds, see how I could contribute. These birds would be my aunts or uncles, and I wondered if one day they would ever turn human like Grandma went from human to bird. I'd only want that if Grandma became a human Grandma again because a bird couldn't care for people babies. I thought it would be best if they all just stayed what they were.

As I was locking Grandma's house up to leave, Kendra appeared behind me on the walk and said hello.

"I followed you here the first day you took me home," she said. "I wanted to see if your Grandma was real or if you were just getting rid of me." Kendra, without asking, walked past me and into Grandma's house. I hadn't seen her, even thought about her, since the day Dad woke, but there she was, in my Grandma's house, minus her favorite accessory, the now-infamous Deirdre.

If Kendra asked, I would tell her Grandma was out of town, in San Diego, maybe somewhere else, that I was going over to take care of her pet canary. But Kendra didn't ask. Still, I showed her the nest and the eggs inside, making sure she kept her distance, not wanting to upset Grandma. Kendra was wearing a very short jean skirt, and as she got on her tiptoes to see inside, the very bottom of her butt came into view. I couldn't believe it: mint green. I wondered if Kendra was wearing the same panties from fourth grade or if mint green was all she wore, like with me and white. I doubted either was true. Sometimes, weird things were just coincidences.

Kendra was impressed by the canary and nest and eggs, an entire wing of my family tree, but after that, I didn't have anything to show her, Grandma's house filled with things for old ladies. We sat down in the living room on the sofa with the plastic covering, and without me asking her to, Kendra brought up Deirdre and Cunny. Deirdre was in awful bad trouble because somehow her mom and dad had found out about the sex. I hadn't told and I knew my dad hadn't, either. Kendra probably didn't believe me—how else could they have found out—but that didn't matter. Deirdre was grounded for forever and neither one of us would see her again until school started.

After running through the channels five times with Grandma's remote, Kendra got bored, and, as plain as day, asked, "Do you want to make out?"

I didn't answer right away because I was so surprised, even though I shouldn't have been. The movie. Her always wanting me to walk her home. Her being there right then. Still, it never crossed my mind, not with my Deirdre titty fetish, not with all the shit that had gone down. But with Kendra offering, it seemed like a good idea. She was one of the more popular girls in our class, pretty, too, an actual blond, and if I started high school with Kendra as my girlfriend, I'd have instant street cred. Even if we didn't last—and we wouldn't—other girls would know I went out with her, that I was the type of guy who could score pretty, popular girls. My lot would be cast: I could be a guy pretty girls liked.

"Sure," I said. "Sounds like a plan."

Kendra leaned in and I leaned in and we kissed, my first, and it was pretty good. Neither one of us had braces, both our breaths were pretty neutral, and without question, neither of us had done this very much. I kissed on her lips for a long time before slipping her anything resembling my tongue, but once I did, she accepted it with enthusiasm, sucking it between her teeth and painting it with her own. Our tongues together felt like a trapped bird, frantic, searching for a way to escape. The whole time, my arms were resting on her shoulders, my fingertips digging in. Kendra just kept her arms crossed in her lap. I opened my eyes a few times, just to make sure I was doing everything right, but as long as Kendra kept going, I couldn't have been doing that bad.

After making out for over fifteen minutes, Kendra told me she had an idea. I wasn't thinking too much at that point, not about ideas, anyway. Kendra stopped kissing and told me to lean back into the sofa, to relax as best as I could because she had this idea. I tried to guess what her idea was. Maybe she wanted to stop kissing and hang out. Maybe she wanted to go to the mall. Maybe she wanted to watch more TV. Girls didn't like sex as much as boys, my dad once said, and Kendra was probably just tired of doing it.

*Doing it*, I heard myself think. Kendra and I had just *done it*.

Kendra's idea involved her kneeling down in front of me, I soon found out, and when Kendra undid the buckle on my belt and loosened my jeans, the picture became a lot clearer. I looked out the window to see if anyone could see in, could make out what she was doing. I saw a dark bird fly by and remembered Grandma, wondering what she would do if she caught us. Recalling her reaction to my earring, I didn't like the thought of her catching me with my pants down.

Kendra put her hands up my shirt and rubbed my flat chest and stomach, brushing my nipples, which made them stick out. Then she hooked her fingers inside the waistband of my underwear and that's when it struck me: I was going to be naked in front of her, naked, and, as of that morning, still completely pubeless. I hadn't been checking *as* closely since Cunny came to town—I'd moved the magnifying glass from the bathroom sink back into the utility drawer—so it was possible I'd missed something.

"Let's see what there is to see," Kendra said.

I could only sit back, close my eyes, and hope for a miracle.

# Victor

A long with the groceries, one day my wife brings home a dummy, a little guy made of wood, a redhead with round cheeks, a high, arching brow, and a goatee. Debbie tells me to unload while she shows Victor around, and that she's getting pretty hungry. She asks what time she should expect dinner.

*Victor?* I ask.

*Hello,* Victor says. *You're better looking than Debbie let on.*

Debbie's hand is inside the dummy's back, but Debbie's mouth doesn't move at all. In fact, she smiles a lot, and at one point during the dummy's speech, she coughs. To the best of my knowledge, Debbie has had no experience with ventriloquism, but now, with ten brown bags and a watermelon on the kitchen floor, she comes off like a pro.

*There's Popsicles in one of those bags,* Debbie says. *Plus I stopped to see your Mom on the way home.*

Debbie disappears into the bedroom, along the way pointing out the paintings she did in college and where the bathroom is. While I have more questions—the least of which is what she was doing at my mother's—those Popsicles are turning to juice. Even stranger, while I'm putting everything away, I find products we've never bought before—yogurt, kiwis, string cheese, a six pack of diet cola. With both Debbie and me lactose intolerant, and neither of us on a diet, I can't imagine who these new items are for, but I put them away just the same.

During dinner, Debbie holds the dummy on her lap, and again, her ventriloquism skills fall nothing short of amazing. While the dummy talks, Debbie takes sips out of her wine, even chews bites of her pork chop. At one point, she interrupts the dummy, then apologizes as he apologizes, making it seem like they're talking at the exact same time, interrupting each other. I clap, tell her I'm impressed, and ask where the dummy came from.

*Victor*, she says, *found my personal ad online.*

Debbie seems to want to play the game out, play it as far as I'll go along with it. I'm not sure how, but Victor is able to use his arms to pick up a fork and put food in his mouth, which must fall into some hole, as in his mouth it stays. Somewhere inside this dummy sits an entire pork chop and a dish of applesauce. He leaves the baked potato untouched, but did waste half a stick of butter and some sour cream. I have no choice but to oblige Debbie's little fantasy and play along, too, lest I be the one who spoils the fun. I've been accused of that in the past, and it's a habit I'm trying to break.

*So Victor*, I say, looking him in his marble-like eyes. *Who do you like in the game tonight?*

Victor finishes chewing a bite and Debbie helps him wash it down by lifting a glass of water—poured just for him—into his wooden mouth, past his straight white wooden teeth.

*I'm not a sports fan*, Victor tells me. *But I'll say the home team, as I'd hate to be rude to my host, jinx the good guys' chances, if you know what I mean.*

For the first time since Debbie's brought this dummy home, I'm irked. I'm not sure if it's because the gag is going on too long or because I hate the snobby tone Debbie has chosen for Victor, as if to tell me *she's* above following sports. Plus, if she's making him sincere, I don't like to be patronized. What kind of way is that to have a dinner conversation? If he's for the Pats, she should just have him tell me he's for the Pats. Like I'm going to judge him for rooting for the opposing team, or worse yet, believe that his cheering is going to affect any outcome. I've always hated guys like that and Debbie knows it.

But I'm probably reading too much into it.

Debbie reminds me that since I cooked, it's her turn to do dishes. She asks me to take Victor down to the rec room, tells me he'd like my collection of beer steins. *He collects zeppelin memorabilia*, she says, *so he knows about stuff from Germany.* I counter with a reminder that the pregame is on, that her tour of the house took a little longer than it should have, and we could maybe look at the steins at halftime. But I'm more than willing to take Victor with me. I'm looking forward to getting my hand in there, make him say the things I want Debbie to hear instead of the other way around. Before I can even ask Debbie to hand him over, Victor interjects.

*I think I'd like to lie down for a while, Deborah. It's been a long day, and Greg's gourmet meal has left me a bit on the drowsy side.*

Debbie looks at me as if it's my choice whether or not Victor can take a nap.

*Game's on in ten*, I say.

Debbie excuses herself from the table, as does Victor, and the two disappear into the guest bedroom. I clear the table, noting that it's taking a bit longer than it should for her to come back. When she finally emerges, she's tiptoeing, as if to be quiet.

*He's a sweet guy*, Deb says, and to keep the gag going, whispers.

*But I think the little bastard likes the Patriots*, I tell her, and give her a wink, a wink that's not returned.

*I told you, it was my job to do the dishes.*

*When do I ever listen to you?*

*Your game is on—you've made that clear.*

*You forgot some things from the store, namely eggs.*

*I'm glad you're OK with him staying. It's big of you to go along with this.*

*I can grab McDonald's in the morning, only I thought we said we weren't going to do that anymore, pick up something on the run.*

Debbie fills the sink, drops Victor's potato into the trash like a bomb. I grab a beer and notice there's only one more in the fridge. I catch myself thinking that I should leave it for Victor in case he gets up and wants to watch the game. I laugh. When Debbie asks why I'm giggling, I tell her the Jets are going to kick the crap out of the Pats, and if anyone thinks differently, his head must be made of wood.

I know why Debbie's doing this, playing this Victor game with me, which is why I have to play along. A few weeks ago, when Debbie was supposed to be at the gym, she came home, her ankle turned, and found me, in our bedroom, with Laura Neumann, the woman who delivers our bottled water. I wasn't naked, Laura wasn't naked, and we weren't even touching. But Laura was sitting on our bed. To any woman who breaks her two-year routine only to find a woman sitting on her husband's bed, her husband just a few feet away and looking startled, this would seem like infidelity. But like I said, Laura's clothes were on, my clothes were on, and Laura's clipboard was in her hands. It was easy for me to tell Debbie that Laura was in our bedroom because she wanted to see if an extra dispenser would fit under a cabinet in our bathroom, that she sat down because she runs up and down people's front walks with five-gallon bottles on her shoulders all day. She was tired, had to run some numbers, and I told her to take a load off. I appeared startled to Debbie because Laura's work clothes were sweaty and Debbie had just done the bedding—I was thinking about the sheets, not some crazy affair with the Culligan lady. As soon as Laura left, Debbie told me she wasn't mad about the sheets, filling me in on what she thought was really going on. I told her she was imagining things. Yes, I'd made comments about Laura before, her tan (probably a farmer's), her thick thighs and lean calves, how it looked like her breasts overtaxed the buttons on her shirt. So I could totally see where Debbie was coming from, and later on, we laughed about it together, made jokes.

Victor's appearance is just the joke taken a step further, the punch line to the online personal she filled out and left on the screen of our laptop. We joke with each other like that: She calls me "Doughboy" sometimes, I dig on her cooking, especially anything from the casserole family. It's how we get along, how any married couple gets along.

And I have to admit, a wooden ventriloquist's dummy is a lot better than Carl the mailman in a thong when I come home early from work. Victor is made of wood, not to mention a snob, maybe even gay, the way he drinks water at dinner and doesn't follow sports. I'll take a wooden gay dummy any day over Carl and his shorty-short blue pants with the black stripe running down the side. As long as Debbie does, too, we won't have a problem.

I'm not sure why, but the next day at work, I tell Charlie about the whole thing, Victor, dinner, Debbie not coming down to say good night before turning in. Charlie is my partner at work, and my best friend, but that doesn't say much, since we don't really see each other off the job. Charlie and I work in old blast furnaces, steel mills and manufacturing plants, mostly, repairing the inner structures when they start to crumble. A company calls our unions—me the Bricklayers, Charlie the Laborers—and the Unions call us. Charlie breaks the old wall down with a sledgehammer, I put in the new wall, then Charlie cleans up. Even though Charlie's in a different union, he is in a union, and knows to follow my lead, to make the job last as long as we can without raising suspicion, without getting a lollygagger rep. It's a good system, a system I plan on exploiting till I'm 55 and Debbie and I can move to Florida. Charlie will find a new bricklayer and we'll lose touch.

*Sounds like you and Deb have some issues to sort out,* Charlie says. *A dummy?*

*The Patriots looked like a bad college team,* I tell him. *Don't they have like ten Pro Bowlers?*

*Maybe's she's trying to tell you something.*

*I don't care how many rings he has, if a guy throws four picks, you sit his ass on the bench till he learns what color his jersey is. But fuck it—they can play Mickey Mouse against the Jets. All the better for us.*

Charlie tells me, in between swings of his hammer, that maybe I should do something special for Debbie tonight, take her to dinner, an artsy movie, maybe dancing. He tells me that Debbie's a pretty lady, that I'm a lucky man, that someone needs to give her the things she deserves. That she's dying for it to be me. I tell him that Debbie's never asked about dancing, never shown any interest, and remind him that he's never taken his wife dancing, either.

*My wife's not the one who brought home a dummy she found online,* man. *And besides, Deb never showed an interest in ventriloquism, yet somehow she's Edgar-fucking-Bergen. Who knows, maybe she's Britney Spears on the dance floor, too. Or Shakira, grabbing herself and humping the floor and shit.*

Technically, since I'm the tradesman, I'm the foreman on our jobs. But I never throw that in Charlie's face—I've never had to. But I'm tempted now. The only reason I don't is because he's sort of right—about the ventriloquism, anyway.

*Red Lobster's having their Shrimp Feast*, I tell Charlie.

Just then, a rat the size of a shoebox runs from the hole Charlie's punched in the wall and I trap it in my mixing bucket.

*Cement shoes?* Charlie asks.

*Oh, yeah*, I say, and instruct Charlie to hand me my trowel.

I didn't think it a possibility, but when I meet Debbie at the restaurant, Victor is perched in her lap. The table holds three place settings, three glasses of water, and the two of them are having a conversation about the movie they went to go see that afternoon, something about an English woman struggling to find her way in a man's world. Everyone in the section is staring at us. Little kids from all over are standing in the aisles, pointing and yelling over toward their parents.

*You look nice*, Debbie says. *I wasn't sure if you'd have time to shower.*

Victor looks up from his menu and says he likes my sweater, that orange, brown, and green are three of his favorite colors. Victor's wearing a white turtleneck with a charcoal sport coat. His hair seems to have some sort of goop in it, as it's pushed back and slick, all curled up in the back.

*You bought him a change of clothes?* I say. Last night, Victor was wearing a long-sleeved button-down, dark blue, I think. I don't remember what kind of pants he had on, and now, I can't see under the tablecloth.

*A little present*, Debbie says. *Victor paid for the movie, and the men's store was right next to the theater. He can't wear the same thing every day, you know—he's not you.*

A woman and a man at the table find this remark very funny, bursting out in a giggle. They clap and ask for Debbie to make Victor say something else. I turn toward them and they put their faces back in their menus.

*Just kidding, honey! You look nice*, Debbie says. She asks me to sit down, across from her and Victor. Before I can do anything—ask Debbie to leave, for instance, and drop Victor in the Dumpster on the way out of the lot—a waitress comes and brings us drinks and salads.

*I took the liberty of ordering for you*, Victor says. *I overheard Debbie playing your message from the machine, touting this "feast" they have going, so I assumed you wanted just that, the Shrimp Feast.*

Debbie digs into her salad with her free hand and Victor does the same. I'm pretty sure she's controlling him lefty, when yesterday, she was using her right. I start to think that she's maybe been secretly taking lessons at night, maybe at the community college, the one we get catalogues from in the mail. I'm not sure when she's been doing this—probably my euchre night—and it makes me feel like we've been leading double lives. Whenever I say I'm going to my folks' to play cards, I go play cards with my folks. When Debbie says she's going to stay in and read, I assume she's reading, in our bed, by herself. I've been playing euchre on Wednesdays for a lot of years, so like Charlie said, who knows what other skills she's acquired in that time? To think that my wife is holding out on me makes me not hungry. Maybe she can fix cars or even mountain-climb? Maybe one night I'll pull around the block, follow her, see if she leaves. But that's crazy talk, and if I have to follow her around, then is she really worth the effort?

I am not a big fan of salad, but pick at it, because I don't want to seem ungrateful to Victor for getting the dressing right, Thousand Island. Then I catch myself for considering the feelings of a piece of wood, one who's wearing nicer clothes than I am, one who remembered to put his napkin on his lap. I push the salad aside and wait for my shrimp. When it comes, I order only one refill, broiled in garlic butter on a wooden skewer, when usually I get three or four extra platters, all fried. Victor's stomach has been whittled flat, I notice, then it hits me: What if Debbie *made* Victor, carved him herself? What if Victor—red hair, perfect manners, chiseled good looks—is what she wants? It would make a lot of sense, but then again, nothing about this makes sense. When the waitress comes at the end of the meal and asks about dessert, I say no, order a water, then watch my wife and her dummy share cheesecake, drizzled in chocolate fudge sauce, what I usually get and Debbie always declines.

I want to kick Charlie in the ribs when he falls over from laughing the next day, telling me he'd give up all his overtime for the year to have seen me at Red Lobster with a ventriloquist's dummy, wearing my orange, brown, and green sweater, all those people watching.

*It would have been enough to see you stop at two plates of shrimp*, he says. *The rest of it, that's just heaven.*

I let Charlie have his fun for five minutes or so, then we get to work. To make my day even better, the hunk of wall we replaced yesterday has fallen in, probably because of the humidity, maybe a rotten bag of mortar. But we have to start over, knock down an even bigger section, make sure the whole wall is stable. If the structure is at all compromised when the stove is lit, the heat could seep through to the gas line and cause an explosion. And that's bad, though it would get us more work; rebricking an entire furnace of this size is usually a two-month job, six days a week, too, maybe ten or twelve hours per.

Charlie does manage to get his barbs in, wondering out loud if wood would be better than bricks, asking if I knew any good carpenters. He tells me I'd look good in a goatee, even smearing one on his face with ash. In a voice that is supposed to be Debbie, I guess, all high and cracking, he says, *Wow, I really love a man in a goatee*, then starts making kissy noises and rubs his arms all over like he's hugging himself, even squeezing where Debbie's breasts would be. I wonder how hard it would be to push Charlie inside the wall I'm building, if I could finish before he came to, if anyone would ever hear him pounding and screaming after I'd gone home. Not like I don't deserve his shit. Serves me right for telling Charlie everything, when honestly, I can't even remember his wife's name, Jill or Julie, something with a J.

At the end of the day, Charlie asks me to go out for a beer later (mentioning that Debbie wouldn't mind the time alone with Victor), but it's euchre night, so I turn him down. *I knew that*, he says. *Just checking.* I can take a joke as much as the next guy, but I think I'd rather spend an evening with the actual Victor and Debbie than any more of Charlie riding me or telling me how lucky I am to have Debbie. When I drop him off at his condo, he does give me one good piece of advice: *Keep a hacksaw by the bed. Just to send a message.*

That night at my folks', I lose big. I'm partnered up with Mom, who is pissed. Dad and Lester, my little brother who lives with them, are kicking our asses. Dad and Lester never beat me and Mom, and in fact, nobody ever beats Mom, whether she's with me, Lester, or Dad. I'm playing that badly. Mom throws her cards down a lot, drinks almost a beer a hand, even says *fuck* a few times, which she almost never does, unless she and Dad are having it out.

We're done way early, Mom wanting nothing more to do with me and my crappy leads. Lester and Dad gloat, a side we rarely ever see. They high-five, they low-five, and they dance around like little girl cheerleaders at a Pop Warner game. Dad goes up to his room—he and Mom sleep separately, have for years—and

Lester goes out to his place above the garage, cigarette in mouth and lighter in hand before he hits the door. Mom, who can barely walk from all the brew, asks me to stay awhile, to have one more with her for the road. Since it's early, I accept, even though I've already had like seven myself, in just a couple of hours.

Mom, always with an agenda, wants to inform me of how good Lester's doing at his new job, but that she misses him when he's gone. He's the baby, her favorite, and no matter what I do, how much I stay out of trouble, he'll always be her favorite. Lester, 39, has been living with our folks for the last five years, a lot of times before that, too, after both divorces, after both rehabs, after, most recently, the DUI that cost him his license and job with UPS. He's scrounged around a lot for work, bagging groceries, sweeping up at a $10 haircut shop, shoveling roadkill for the city. But recently, Dad got him in at GM, working the line, a real backbreaker, putting doors the size of easy chairs on SUVs. Dad thought Lester was ready to handle the pressure, that this job was the answer. *He and your father drive in together, come home together*, Mom says, as if to imply Lester can't get into any trouble if Dad drags him around by the hand. When I remind Mom that Dad only has a few months to retirement, she finishes her beer and gets up to get another. She asks if I want one more (again), but I give her mine, only a sip or two deep, still cold.

*He'll either be ready to do it on his own, or he won't. If he is, then maybe he can talk about getting his own place. If not, then he'll just fuck it up, end of story. He can't sit on your father's lap and steer forever, you know—sooner or later, he's going to have to work the pedals, too.*

Mom is more than half in the bag at this point, but I still have to ask her: *How long have you been working on that line?*

*Heard it on Oprah*, Mom says. *I watch a lot of TV now, without Lester around to talk to.*

I tell Mom that I should drop over more, maybe twice a week instead of once, and she pats my hand, tells me I have a wife, a beautiful wife, and my job is to take care of her, that I should think about putting my storm windows in this weekend, that you never know when the cold will come. It's only September, a week after Labor Day, but this reminds me to ask about Debbie's visit, her post-shopping stop-in. As soon as I ask, Mom looks at me like I just screwed up another hand of euchre.

*Maybe she meant* her *mother*, Mom says. She stares me down, knows that I'm serious, that I think Debbie's been to visit her in the last couple of days. That Debbie lied. *But I wish she'd drop by—the store's just around the corner. We could have coffee, maybe a beer. Tell her I said hello.*

Soon after, I help Mom up to her room, put her under her covers in her bed, kiss her on the forehead. If she hadn't been drinking, I maybe would have asked her about Victor, about what it all means, but then again, it's probably good that I don't. As hard a time as Charlie gave me at work, Mom would probably be worse, lecture me on fulfilling my husbandly duties, then offer to let me live at home for a while, share the garage with Lester until things with Debbie work out. Mom can be awful when she's drunk, way too momly, but she's Mom, and she can say whatever she wants to me and it would be fine.

When I get home, the house is dark, which isn't unusual, as it's almost midnight. If she remembers, Debbie will leave the stove light on for me on Wednesdays, help me get across the table and chairs, assuming I'd had a few. With Lester's list of problems, I'm not sure why she fosters my once-a-week binging, but again, that's the way we deal with each other. I have my things, she has hers. We're married, and that's what married couples do, cover.

But lying about visiting my Mom isn't one of those things that we do. That's covering, but not for me, for her. It's odd, because she could have said she was anywhere—the bank, the post office, the library, even at the store the whole time. It wasn't like I was timing her. She could have come home an hour later and I wouldn't have said anything. But she chose to tell me she stopped at my mother's, that the Popsicles were melting, that I needed to put them in the freezer while she took her fucking puppet on a tour of the house. It was deliberate and even worse, she had to know I'd ask Mom about it, a few days later. Tonight. And she was right. But why?

Whether she's asleep or not, I'm going to wake her up and ask. She won't want to talk to me while I'm drunk—leaving a light on is one thing, fighting with me is another—but I don't care. She brought this upon herself. She has to pay.

Up in our bedroom, I see the light under the bathroom door and hear the shower. It is two hours past her bedtime, and even though I'm an hour earlier than usual, I doubt Debbie takes showers this late every Wednesday. I think to myself that she doesn't do all that much during the day, cooks and cleans, gets the groceries, so why would she need to shower so late, right before bed? I turn the bathroom door handle, wanting to surprise her, but find it locked, so I sit down on the bed, willing to wait for her to finish.

Lo and behold, I find Debbie asleep next to me, under the covers, stirring, a smile on her face as if she's having a good dream. Even stranger than taking a shower so late at night, Debbie has taken a shower, and has left the light on and the water running, the door locked. Maybe that explains it somehow—she got locked out of the bathroom, hours ago, with the light on and the shower still spewing water. She knows I have a way of jiggling open the door, using a steak knife, and she's going to have a laugh with me, say something ridiculous about paying me back for the water and electricity she's wasted. She will smell good, she will smell clean, and if I wasn't drunk, we might have sex. The job ended today and I have nowhere to be in the morning, no plans except maybe the storm windows. Only I *am* drunk, and my wife will not have sex with me while I'm drunk.

Just as I'm about to wake Debbie, ask her about her visit to Mom's, I hear the water in the shower stop, the bathroom curtain open, someone step out.

Debbie is not alone here—we are not alone here. There is an intruder in our house, but more than likely, not really an intruder: an invited guest. I need only one guess as to who it is, what he's been doing in my house. And I'm pretty sure he's not going to like what I'm going to do about it.

# Cool

The first boy my sister ever slept with had a ferret named Fonzie. When our dad was at work and Mom was at church or down at the store, this guy would come by with the thing on a little leash and sit on our front porch, letting the ferret work its magic. Some guys came by with cars, some guys just sat on the porch and combed their hair. This guy had a ferret, and as stupid as it seems now, it worked. At least with my big sister.

Even though he stank like wet feet, Fonzie was pretty cool to me. I was ten or eleven at the time and had never heard of ferrets, let alone had one crawl up my shirtsleeve or down my back. My sister was sixteen, just turned, and she'd never seen a ferret, either, I think, but here this guy was, tan and curly blond and out of high school at least two years, his teeth whiter than headlights. He was as cool as I could imagine. The last boyfriend she had wasn't old enough to drive, and, with his thick, black glasses and thick lips, looked like Charlie the Tuna from the tuna can. My sister didn't go out with him very long, and I knew as a fact she didn't have sex with him because he kept calling after she broke it off. Over the next few years, I learned that boys would stop calling once she went all the way, or would never be home when she tried them. Even today, I would have thought it just the opposite. I started thinking that maybe something was wrong with my sister, that she didn't have everything in the right place, but that's not the kind of thing a little brother wants to imagine.

While I let Fonzie run about the railing spokes and through hedges in front of the lawn, Ken—that was the guy's name—would sit at the top of the stairs and tell my sister how pretty she was, and after a few visits, sneak her pecks on the lips. I would say things like "Aww!" when I'd catch them, and Ken would smile at me and wink, then tell me to bring Fonzie over to him. Ken could make his ferret do all sorts of tricks, most of them involving Fonzie hanging from his leash and swinging around. I always thought that Fonzie would choke or his neck would break, but ferrets didn't have bones in their neck, Ken told me, just blood and tissue. It didn't sound right to me, but after regrouping, Fonzie kept coming back for more, blood and tissue and all.

Once when Ken was over, Dad came home early from work. He was a crane repairman at a steel mill, and that morning, a man he'd know for a long time had fallen into one of the vats of molten metal, evaporating instantly. Half the mill closed. When Dad pulled up, Ken was doing one of his rope tricks with Fonzie, wrapping the leash around his belt buckle and suspending him between his legs, just swinging the little guy back and forth against his knees. Dad got out of his car and told me and my sister to go into the house. I told my father that ferrets didn't have bones, that Fonzie would be OK, and he told me again to go into the house, only this time he yelled it, slamming the door to his Buick Regal for emphasis. My sister didn't say anything, but listened from inside the front door, ear pressed against wood, while I looked out the picture window. Ken was walking backwards away from my father, who was turning red. Ken looked happy, smiling and putting his hands up as if my dad had a gun, pulling Fonzie along by his belt. Dad came inside when Ken was out of sight and told me to go back out. I don't know what he said to my sister after that, but Ken never came to the house again, even when Dad and Mom separated and Dad moved across State Line Road to Indiana, right by the mill where he worked.

I never saw Fonzie the ferret again, but I did see Ken one more time. My sister got her driver's license soon after Dad left, and Mom would send her and me to the store because she had to get a job and we needed to help out. On the way to the Sterk's, my sister would make stops, sometimes at a girlfriend's, sometimes to buy things at other stores, but one time at these apartments above the pharmacy where we got our prescriptions filled. We took the stairs in the back, and when my sister knocked on his door, Ken answered and let us in. I, of course, wanted to know where Fonzie was, and Ken told me he'd had an accident, that he'd drowned in the toilet and went straight to Ferret Heaven. I wanted to cry, but with Ken there, I didn't, just held it in.

After we talked for a while—Ken drank a beer and put on a rock record—he gave me three one-dollar bills and told me to go down to the pharmacy, count how many different kinds of candy bars there were, and buy, for him, what I thought were the five heaviest. Then I could buy myself whichever one I wanted, but he told me to make sure I got a heavy one. "You don't want to get ripped off, little man. Take your time."

Even at eleven, I think I knew what was going on in Ken's apartment. I wasn't four, and wasn't that into candy, and had already started sprouting pubic hair in my pits. I went to the magazine section instead of counting anything and pretended to look at a *Sports Illustrated*, but really was trying to get up my nerve to pick up a dirty magazine. They were on a different rack than the other periodicals, right next to the pharmacist's counter, and because I was kind of a sickly little kid, I'd been in there with my mom enough times to believe I'd be recognized. Three dollars wasn't enough to buy a magazine and anything else, so I bought a strawberry Charleston Chew and five packs of basketball cards, then went and sat on the stairs outside. I looked through the cards and only knew one of the players, Dr. J, and put him in my pocket. I threw the rest on the ground, hoping someone would come by and tell me to pick them up just so I could ignore them. That day, for the first time, I wanted to look cool.

Sooner or later, I knew my sister would come down to find me, probably yell at me for taking Ken's money and not coming back with any candy. I didn't care. We were supposed to be grocery shopping, and if she was mean to me, I could just tell on her. I took a long time to eat the Charleston Chew, unwrapping the whole thing and throwing the pink paper down by the basketball cards. Chocolate coating got all over my fingers and probably my face, and I smeared it in my pants and T-shirt. While I chewed and chewed, I fantasized about how mad Mom would be, how I'd have to explain how I got chocolate all over, who gave me the money for it, what took us so long at the store. When I got tired of hearing Mom's voice in my head, I imagined another man falling into a vat of glowing orange steel, maybe hanging from an I-beam for a while, my dad screaming for him to grab his hand, just about reaching it before the man lost his grip. Everyone would be sent home early again, and maybe Dad would have to get a prescription filled, some pills a doctor wanted him to take so he wouldn't be sad.

Just then, a Regal like my dad's drove by, maroon with a white top and white interior, but it wasn't Dad, it was a black guy with his family, listening to the Sox game and driving in the wrong direction from our house. I licked my fingers, and for a moment, I wished that the black man was my dad, that I was in the back of the car, smearing chocolate on the white seats, turning my neck and seeing some messy white kid sitting outside a pharmacy. I would wonder who the kid was, why he was alone. I'd know that when I got home, my dad would see the mess I'd made, then he'd slam his door and tell my mom and sister to go inside. Then he'd yell for me to leave, expecting me never to come back.

# In My Lover's Bedroom

**M**y lover is hiding old men in the recesses of her bedroom, but if you ask her about it, she'll deny it every time. Despite what she claims, I discover men in her closet, men in her armoire, men skulking behind the vanity or crouched in the trunk at the foot of her bed. The men act pleasant, appear comfortable and content, and all of them seem to know my name, offering salutations and good words in abundance. To pass the time, the men read newspapers, listen to transistor radios, and some of them, if it's nice outside, fit in nine holes of golf. When I ask about my lover, they change the subject, remind me who won some game, ask if my career's taking off. When I ask what they're doing in my lover's bedroom, reading and resting and recreating in general, they act like they can't hear me, and if I press, they start speaking a foreign language, albeit very poorly. Aside from random pleasantries, the old men go about their business, keep to themselves, and at worst, tell good off-color jokes.

The problem with the old men is, I only find them when I'm alone, when my lover is in the kitchen, in the bathroom, home late from her job at the club. I've asked her many times why she keeps men in her dresser drawers, and her answer is the same, every time: *Why are you going through my drawers?*

When I open said drawer to show her, the man has disappeared. The first time this happened, my lover thought it was funny, some sort of dry humor I'd never before demonstrated. On the second occasion, she was less amused. She assured me she had no other lover, she wasn't married, and as far as she knew, she had no plans for that to change. On the third try, she suggested I leave, forcing me to apologize, to admit I'd taken a joke too far. Since then, I've decided to keep the men to myself, to go to them for answers. When I inquire as to why they won't let my lover in on the joke, I get the *What?* treatment, the toggle of an imaginary microphone in their ears. It almost makes me think I'm onto something.

Back in grad school, this guy from Kenya lived in the office we shared in our department's building. He didn't tell me, or anyone else, but he slept on the floor, ate at the cafeteria, and showered at the student rec center. Roger was a pleasant enough guy, a wife and three kids back in Africa, a job with his country's state department on hold. Really, he had everything I wanted out of my own life, only he was stuck in America for twenty-one months, earning a political science master's, too poor to fly home to visit. For the longest time, I didn't figure his secret out, not until I dropped by in the middle of the night to pick up some papers. The office was dark, Roger was sleeping on the floor, and he scared the shit out of me when I flipped on the light. I asked if everything was OK and he told me he'd been pulling an all-nighter, that he'd been resting and just nodded off. I wished him a good evening and didn't think much of it, even admired him for his dedication. By the time I got home, I started thinking about the logistics, how I'd never seen him leave campus, how he was always in the men's room, washing a dish, a cup, or his face. I decided to watch Roger after that, follow him around campus, and it only took a day to confirm what I'd suspected. By that time, graduation was two weeks away, and Roger, who had fooled everyone for so long, deserved a reprieve. My own life was a mess at the time, so I had no right to judge. One bad break, an emergency this or that, and I would've been evicted from my apartment and on the floor next to him, making small talk, wondering what he said when custodial came to empty the trash.

One day I decide to make the old men some offers. When I find one of them whittling under the bed, I invite him into the other rooms, ask him if he'd like something to drink, a soft place to sit, better light. He could whittle to his heart's content, watch a little TV, tell me a bit about himself. I've taken the man off guard, I can tell, and after what appears to be serious deliberation, he kindly turns me down, says he has to get back to his turtle, which I guess is what he's busy whittling. My lover is out of town on this night, unaware of my presence in her apartment, though she's entrusted me with a key. Alone, I take advantage of the time to think, to settle matters with all the old men. I check on the whittler every so often, every time I can think of something new to lure him out of hiding: a sandwich, a cigarette, a sharper whittling knife. Every time, I'm turned down. I try other hiding spaces in the room, the closet, the grandfather clock, the dressers—thirteen drawers in all—and make similar offers to other old men, every one of their interests piqued, though not enough to emerge from their current locations. Frustrated, I move to other rooms, search for other men, maybe a different type of man, but fail. I return to my lover's bedroom and spend the night there, in the middle of the bed, on top of the covers. Within seconds, I doze off. The old men, if anything, are courteous of the hour, and I sleep as solidly as I ever remember sleeping.

Waking refreshed and rejuvenated, I make a bold decision. When my lover returns from her trip, she will find the key to her apartment in her mailbox, a note attached explaining my departure. The note is longer than I want it to be, but in it I detail every way in which she has wronged me, every way she could have salvaged what we had. Before I slip the key and note into her slot, I take a deep breath and recall the vacation we took together, not long after we'd met, an island-hopping cruise in the South Pacific. It was two weeks of drinks with umbrellas, necklaces made of shells, and walks on nude beaches. As the boat pulled back into the San Diego harbor, my lover put her hand on my back, kissed me on the cheek, thanked me for the wonderful time. She told me she could see herself growing old with me, together, that we could have a home.

Since that moment, I've tried to hold my lover to her promise, but have only seen her move further away. As soon as I drop the note and the key into the box, when I feel the tinny thud of the brass striking aluminum, I imagine my lover's call when she returns. With coaxing, I'll remind her of her pledge, repeat what she said on the ship about growing old together. I'll speak the words she spoke, imitating her conniving whisper, and no matter how good I am at being her, she will accuse me of another odd joke, deny she'd ever said such things, insist I admit that I made it all up.

# Prison Romance

**M**y cellmate and I spend a lot of time talking about love. You get around to it when you're inside, just like everything else. I describe my wife, old girlfriends, plus the ones I always wanted but never had the guts to ask out. Rollo, whispering from the bottom bunk, says my wife's a whore and I should get over her. I'm only three weeks into a five-to-seven, he says, and unless she's in a coma, she's gonna get her some action, probably sooner than later. Rollo's a lifer, killed a guy he found in bed with his fiancée, so I see his angle, what the deal is with the whore remark. It doesn't help his parole was nixed the day I showed, his next hearing five years away, minus our three weeks together. Still, I know from my first stint inside, Rollo's twelve years in have earned him the right to call June a whore. Plus, I'm a heavy sleeper, and heavy sleepers just shouldn't argue.

What I don't tell Rollo, what I've never told anyone, is how June's a virgin, even after six years with me. Good-looking, twenty-five, but still no sex—not what's generally considered the deal-maker. We tried a couple times, and once we were close, but I was drunk. Then that was that. It was an excuse, like all the others, but throw in no job, and recently, the robberies, and it didn't add up for me. Not in that way.

Rollo's views on love don't apply to him, of course, because his wife wasn't a whore—she got *raped*. The way Rollo tells it, he faked leaving for work, drove around the block, and after he'd gone just two laps, a pickup was parked in his driveway. When he went inside, he heard his wife screaming, and as fast as he could pull the scissors from the utility drawer, it was over. Once—and only once—I asked him what'd made him drive around the block, why he didn't just go to work that day. Rollo said, "That's exactly what they asked me when I was up on the witness stand."

During June's visits we talk through two-inch-thick glass, using telephones with two-second delays. We hear what we say after we say it, lips not matching sounds. A guard monitors everything, editing anything inappropriate. I want to tell June she looks nice, her sweater green like her eyes, her hair in a bun, like a schoolteacher. Since we're not alone, I don't, instead mentioning the trailers in the yard—for conjugal visiting. I tell her I miss her and wait for her reply. Her mouth opens, two seconds pass, but no sound comes through. I want to believe it's the guard behind this, cutting her off. For the next two seconds, I wonder if it's the June of now who's sitting quiet in front of me or the June of just a moment ago. If I could take back what I said. If it wasn't already too late.

# The Magic of Oil Painting

In 1978, my father bought an oil painting of a lion for two dollars at a flea market and nailed it to the wall above my bed. The painting had a cheap pine frame surrounding a sky-blue background that may have been the sky, or just by coincidence the background color. The lion's head in the painting proudly stared off at a random point. I imagined a gazelle or a zebra next to my dresser on the opposite wall, standing still and unaware, eating my socks and underwear like tall savannah grasses. The odd thing about the painting, though, was that it depicted a maneless lion, a lioness, a girl cat, in a twelve-year-old boy's room. Pete Rose slid headfirst to its left; a sad hobo clown juggled three bowling pins to its right. Whatever possessed my dad to see a girl lion painting and spend two bucks on it, I don't know, but my dad had done a lot of impulsive things of late—the juggling clown included—so when I came home from school and saw the lioness on my wall, it really didn't surprise me.

Since Mom had cheated on Dad with Oscar the butcher, Dad spent a lot more time and energy on my sisters and me, trying to make up for what I would call incompetent fathering. Not abusive, not neglectful, not bad—just sort of goofy. For instance, Dad couldn't perform basic dad functions, like play baseball or even drive a car, so more often than not, playing catch resulted in his nose swelling red, and bus trips landed us in the bad part of town, mugged of our return bus fare and forced to call one of cheating Mom's relatives. He tripped over his own feet a lot, too, though he tried to pass it off as if he had done so on purpose. Once he ate all our Halloween candy. I loved my dad, and so did my twin little sisters, but maybe in the way you love a character on TV: the crazy neighbor with the once-an-episode catch phrase, or the police sergeant with heartburn in his big heart. One of the Sweathogs, maybe. Dad proved steady that way, always good for well-intentioned laughs, but never to be relied upon to carry the whole show.

Whatever Dad did, the paintings, the failed trips to the museum, pink tubes socks mismatched and balled in the wrong drawer, he was trying his best. Mom, when she left, left us completely, moving in with Oscar at his apartment behind his butcher shop, one room and a kitchen that fumed with the aroma of meat, bloody footprints leading to the bed where she had cuckolded my whole family. Or so I pictured it. She didn't return our calls, never snuck back to get her things, and once, when I walked down to Oscar's to confront her, she refused to even see me. Oscar pretended not to know what I was talking about, then asked me to buy something or leave. For a while, I wondered if Mom really was in the back, if maybe we'd imagined the whole thing and Mom was dead or visiting Aunt Jane in Snow Shoe. But I knew Oscar was lying about knowing where Mom was for sure when Dad got home that night and asked me not to go to the butcher shop anymore, that he could take care of "the Mom situation" himself. Not five minutes later, I heard him swearing and bolting out to the car, Kellie and Callie still at gymnastics, Dad forgetting to pick them up at the same time he was forgetting he couldn't drive, that he had to run the entire way.

The day after I went to find Mom at Oscar's, I found the lioness on the wall in my room. Like I said, it didn't really shock me, and so I wouldn't hurt Dad's feelings, I left the painting where it was, figured I'd get used to it, or if I was lucky, see it replaced with something else Dad took a shine to, maybe even a girl in a bathing suit. Farrah Fawcett was on everybody's wall, but the Lynda Carter Wonder Woman was growing on me.

During dinner that night, Dad asked what I thought of the painting and I told him I liked lions, even the girl kind, and wanted to know if he'd painted it himself. It was the most preposterous question ever asked in the history of questions, as ridiculous as if I'd asked if he made the Salisbury steak in our TV dinners. But it made Dad laugh, blush a little, too. While we ate our pudding, made with Squirt instead of milk, he told my sisters he was going to build them a new dollhouse, that their old one was falling apart, that maybe their dolls could all have their own rooms. He joked he would find a little pommel horse for them to do gymnastics on, along with a mini-lion painting to put on one of the walls. My sisters seemed to like the idea, and for what it was worth, I told my father I wanted to help, that I'd always wanted to learn to work with wood. We did the dinner dishes from that night, all day, and the day before, then watched TV until it was bedtime. Dad tucked in the twins and even let me stay up extra to watch Carson's monologue, something I'd never been allowed to do when Mom was still living at home. All in all, things weren't that bad.

Before I fell asleep that night, I heard my father on the telephone, trying to keep his voice down, not realizing the actual thinness of our house's walls. When I heard him say "Lucille," I knew he was talking to Mom, doing pretty well at first, speaking like a lawyer in negotiations, asking where the deed to the house was, chiding her for cutting off everyone's health insurance by quitting her job at the jar lid factory. Before long, though, he was basically begging for her to come back, using me and my sisters as bait, bait Mom wasn't biting on because I think I heard him cry after he hung up.

Dad turned the TV back on and I thought about getting up to talk to him, but instead I stayed where I was and looked around my room. A strip of white shone under my door but disappeared when Dad switched off the light in the hall. The moon through the blinds gave me a striped view of my bedroom door and the sad hobo clown, but I couldn't see much else. Pete Rose, right next to the window, slid undetected into pitch black. The lioness, which should have been watching over me— at least that's what I imagined Dad going for—was completely gone, but if I squinted, I could still make out her outline in the blue background. For a while, I focused on the outline, tried to remember what the lioness looked like, but before long, I only saw the background for what it was—the place where the lioness was supposed to be. I fell asleep that way, my head tilted back, my eyelids failing, staring up into a misshapen patch of sky-blue maybe-not sky. In a lot of ways, that blue patch in the background, the bright emptiness, the mystery, was better than the lioness herself.

# My Lover's Name

One Saturday last June, my lover lost her name. Unbuttoning each other's shirts, her working up, me working down, the feeling hit me first, a weird air of unfamiliarity.

"Who are you?" I had to ask.

My lover stopped, stared up, and answered, "I don't know."

We examined what we did know. We knew where she lived, that she was a catalogue librarian, and that we were indeed lovers, fond of each other for some time. What we faced was a complete absence of nomenclature, a hole in the informal and interpersonal language, a person without a name, and without everything associated with such a luxury.

At first, we thought perhaps we'd only forgotten my lover's name, due to maybe too much wine, a bump on the headboard, or a long, tedious week for each of us at work. After an hour of not being able to remember, she called her friends, and they couldn't remember, either. We called her mother, who wasn't home, and her estranged father in Oregon, who answered but had nothing to offer. No one I knew was even aware she existed, a secret we agreed was best. We considered the whole dilemma a practical joke, but that didn't make any sense: There were too many people involved, including ourselves. And really, it wasn't all that funny.

Our next plan was to consult places my lover's name was printed, permanent records that no one could forge. Inside the Valentine's Day card on her nightstand, my name was still at the bottom, but it simply read, "Dear          ," at the top. Next we consulted the phone book, again finding nothing. "Maybe you're unlisted?" I posited, but my lover was quick to remind me that the phone book was how I'd originally tracked her down, first seeing her now-elusive handle on her name tag at the library. We were about to try another avenue, her driver's license, anything in her purse, but on a hunch, I flipped to the front of the directory. Sure enough, on the line before the As, to the right of a blank space, sat her number. It was the only nameless entry in the book. At that point, we could no longer deny what had happened. Her name was gone.

"That ex with your name on his biceps is having a good day," I joked, and that lightened the mood just a bit, but didn't solve our problem.

Of course, we tried giving my lover her name back, or at the very least, renaming her, not knowing what her name was to begin with. This proved as fruitless as trying to remember. *Veronica*, for example, was a good name for a lover, but as soon as I applied it to mine specifically, I'd forget it. This kept happening, too. *Roxanne*, I'd think, always wanting to date a Roxanne, but then, *Poof!* The name would vanish when I associated it with my lover's face. Oddly enough, some names did work, in the sense I wouldn't forget them. We found a book of baby names she had on her shelf, and when I would read "Bertha," I was able to look in her eyes, say it aloud. But soon it was clear my lover was *not* a Bertha, that it just didn't fit; I could call her *Bertha* because it wasn't her name and never could be. Anything that sounded good would vanish, and any name that didn't sound good would stick around until we nixed it. Out of options, I thought it was time to give up, to move on. So we did.

Not having a name, my lover soon found, had its good points and bad. The library could no longer cut her a proper check, but instead paid her in cash, tax free, with a stoic promise to keep things "hush-hush." Telemarketers stopped calling, but after a while, figured out that "resident" or "lady of the house" would work just as well. While my lover realized she could never again win a raffle, she could also never be summoned for jury duty. "I wish this'd happened back in school," she noted. "I hated being called on. I never knew the answers." Overall, I suggested to my lover that she'd come out ahead, especially with no taxes, but she teetered on the border, the mystery eating at her more than it did me.

Personally, I found that my lover losing her name had a bigger upside than down. Communication, for one, became swift and easy. E-mail was impossible, text messages, too, our phone calls cut to their chase each and every time. Not being able to refer to her, or worry about forgetting to, made me, in many ways, a better man, and a better lover. For the first time since my lover had become my lover, I felt relaxed. My lover's name, whatever it was, seemed to carry with it a lot of baggage, as if our problems were ones of identity. The fights were gone. The crying fits, too. Unreasonable requests disappeared altogether. Perhaps her hatred of politics and mine of opera were called "Sally." Without having to think, I felt like I knew what I wanted and was able to express it. As a result, my lover and I shifted into automatic, just doing what we wanted to do, when we wanted to, no pressure to go in any particular direction. We just *were*, and that's all I ever wanted, even before she lost who she was.

Better yet, my wife, Rhonda, a woman with an internal sense about truth, ceased her suspicion. Records of my affair became scant while the time I'd been spending away was whittled down, impromptu rendezvous more difficult than ever. Meddling questions were replaced by pecks on the cheek and pats on the rear, and some of the time I'd been spending with my lover I spent with my wife, out of necessity, out of convenience, and eventually, out of the need to call someone by her name. I'd never been one to scream out in passion, but I'd started doing so, over and over, "Rhonda! Rhonda! Rhonda!"

As happy as I felt about what, in my eyes, was a fortified arrangement, my lover fielded the opposite reaction. The fighting returned, along with the crying jags. In addition, my lover began hinting at a dwindling interest on my part, citing a communication gap, as well as blatant disrespect for her person, which, as she described, was all she had left—the *person*. Her complaints stopped short of outright accusation, never telling me her situation was my fault, but she did use the phrase "You're taking me for granted," and more than once in any given conversation. In many ways, that was much worse than just blaming me—or me actually being responsible.

Soon, calls I made to my lover went unanswered, and for a while, I wondered if something had gone awry, an unpaid bill, a cat-chewed cord, or worse, a slip in the tub, blood coating the mosaic tile in a sheen. Eventually, I realized she was fine—aside from the lack of a name—and that she had chosen to ignore me, end our affair without giving me a vote. I couldn't say I blamed her, or wouldn't have done the same, but severing the relationship so suddenly, and without warning, left me with an array of emotions, feelings I'd never had before. I wanted to be angry, I wanted to miss her, but I couldn't figure out which. It was something new to me— something unexpected, something unwelcome. Something I couldn't quite put my finger on.

Not as suddenly, memories of my lover faded like her name, everyday thoughts, things I *had* taken for granted. Gone. One day I couldn't remember her birthday, and then I had no idea what color her eyes were. Soon the tone of her voice disappeared, too, and I started replacing it with Rhonda's, blurring my lover's face with my wife's. This wasn't right at all. I had heard from a friend of a friend that my lover was no longer at the library, so I began to wonder if my lover herself was disappearing, that one day I wouldn't remember her, no matter how hard I tried, because *she* was gone. I felt a sense of panic, but soon forgot what it was I'd gotten so upset about in the first place.

Soon these anxieties ceased as well. Once in a while, I'd run across something that triggered a ghost, a song she'd put on a CD, an actress in a commercial with the same hair, a woman with her perfume standing in front of me on the El. At these moments, it seemed like my lover's name was at the tip of my tongue—if I could just concentrate, I'd be able to remember. But a man could get lost trying to regain what was gone, and it was best to let it go. That was easier for me than for her, I was sure: All I had to do was *allow* myself to forget. Soon I even thought about finding a new lover, one with a name I could never lose, could never want to. She would be everything my old lover was, possess all the traits that made me happy. It would be like she knew me before I knew her, understand who I wanted to be, and most of all, she would accept it all. Love me for who I already was, who I would always be.

# Nectarine Pie

*Nectarines are essentially the same fruit as peaches;
the primary difference is that nectarines are smooth-
skinned and peaches are fuzzy.*
    —Nectarine Fruit Facts Page Information

We were driving down through Georgia, Interstate 75, talking about killing and eating each other, when the subject
of nectarines came up. I was in the back seat and, since
Chattanooga, was holding a full tank of piss. I couldn't be sure
if we'd passed Atlanta or not—I'd fallen asleep after crossing
the state line—but I knew I wanted Fred to stop the car, let me
hit the head. I'd volunteer to drive, buy a box of donuts for the
road. I'd even buy dinner, if dinner cost less than $20 for three
people, which seemed unlikely.

"We stopped when you were asleep," Fred said when I asked.
"I called your name, even shook you, but you didn't wake up."

Fred was either lecturing me on heavy sleeping or he
wasn't going to stop. I hoped it was the former.

"Have a peach," Estrella said. Her eyes were dark and
full like coal, or prunes, eager, like she really wanted me to have
a peach. A full bushel of peaches sat on the floor behind Fred's
seat. I'd been awake for over an hour and never noticed them
sitting there, not even the smell. Estrella continued: "They're
not sweet—someone just picked them, didn't give them time to
get juicy. But you can have as many as you want."

I thought about that, eating so much of something that
wasn't good. Fred asked me to pass him six peaches and he

proceeded to eat them, the first thing I'd seen either of them eat all day.

"I don't think I'll kill you now," I said to Fred and Estrella. Estrella laughed, closing her eyes. Fred threw a pit out the window. His face was covered with juice and a stringy piece of peach meat sat at the tip of his collar. I wasn't sure if he'd heard me, that I wouldn't kill them, because he didn't say anything. He just put another peach up to his mouth.

"It's a good thing you're not going to kill us," Fred said a few miles later, finishing that peach. "We only picked you up so we could kill you."

The yellow-and-black sign for the peach-cured ham made me hungry, but not hungry enough to eat a peach. I had to go the bathroom so badly that the thought of eating something made of so much water made my bladder hurt even more. I was convinced we were well past Atlanta and almost in Florida, three states and half a day since I'd peed. There would have been billboards for things in Atlanta if we were coming up on it still. Instead, there were only billboards for things made of peaches and pecans, but mostly peaches. Bushels of peaches, like the one half-empty next to my feet, but also peach cobbler, peach pie, peach candy, peach salsa, and peach ice cream, too. That's what Georgia had to offer the world, peaches. I wondered if Georgians, the people from Georgia, ate as many peaches as they sold. I pictured a family sitting down for a Sunday dinner, a mom in a nice house dress—she looked like Estrella—bringing out a roasting pan, and the dad with the horn-rimmed glasses and the white button-down shirt—Fred—opening it to a steaming goulash of peaches and pecans. The children smiled and inhaled the aroma, each with a fork in one hand, a knife in the other. I'd never been to Florida before but wondered if it was the same with oranges there—orange everything. It probably wasn't, but then again, I'd lived in Chicago for most of my life, and people ate a lot of pizza and hot dogs. Still, Illinois wasn't the Hot Dog State or the Deep Dish State. They were the Land of Lincoln and that seemed honorable. Better than peaches everywhere, kids taking field trips to orchards instead of Springfield to rub Lincoln's nose. It hit me then how I couldn't remember the taste of pecans at all, though I knew I'd had them, at some point, probably in candy bars. Peaches, though, I could taste as we drove. I couldn't *not* taste them. They were part of the air.

"You'd taste good with peach syrup drizzled over you," Fred yelled back to me. Georgia was in the eastern part of the time zone, and I figured that it had to be near 8 o'clock with this amount of light in the middle of July.

"We'll have to stop for some before we get to Florida," Estrella said. "I don't think he'd taste as good with orange marmalade."

I thought it was funny, how Estrella was thinking the same thing I was, about the oranges and Florida. The hitchhiker/murder jokes were still funny, too, in a ghoulish way, something we'd started in Kentucky, Fred insisting they were the ones with bad intentions, claiming they'd kill me before I'd kill them. Cannibalism wasn't too far behind, having come up somewhere around Knoxville, the last time I'd gone to the bathroom.

Fred, finishing off the umpteenth peach and tossing the pit out the window, made this revelation: "How come there's not all this stuff but with nectarines instead?"

We were silent. I watched the billboards as we drove and thought I saw a road sign that said, "Tampa 111."

"What do you mean, *nectarines*?" Estrella said.

Fred looked back at me for another peach, but there weren't any. He'd eaten the entire bushel, minus at least one, the one Estrella bit into to determine they weren't sweet.

Fred said, "There's peach pie, and apple pie, and strawberry and blueberry pie. There's raspberry, even something called 'gooseberry' that I don't personally believe in. There's banana cream pie and coconut cream pie, and I'm pretty sure I had a pineapple pie once, somewhere out West. There's even pumpkin pie—you can buy it anywhere—but you'd never eat pumpkin alone, just in pie. It's basically garbage, good for jack-o'-lanterns and pig slop. Rhubarb's the same way."

"But no nectarine pie," Estrella said. "Or nectarine anything. Huh."

"Why do you think that is?" Fred said. Nobody answered, not out loud.

This was not sitting well with me, either. For some reason, I became angry, angry for nectarines, how they'd gotten the shaft. Maybe it was the pain in my groin from having to piss, but I was becoming emotional. Why wasn't there any nectarine pie? Or candy? Or popsicles? Yogurt or baby food, either?

"Nectarines are better than peaches," I said several miles later. Both Fred and Estrella turned around. It was the first thing I'd said since asking to go to the bathroom some hours earlier, in Macon, I think. They looked at me for as long as Fred could keep his eyes off the road.

"How so?" Fred said. He said it like he wanted me to go on, that he knew I was agreeing with him, not as if to start an argument.

I considered saying that I'd tell him only if he stopped so I could go to the bathroom, just on the side of the road, near a ditch, maybe a place where we could get something to eat besides peaches. But I wanted to tell him about nectarines as much as I wanted those other things. More.

"Nectarines are smoother, no fuzz. I hate the fuzz on peach, how it tickles my lips—plus it makes me feel like I'm eating hair. They're usually darker than peaches, too, which means they're sweeter. Hey—why isn't there a color called 'nectarine,' either, or a Crayola crayon? There just isn't. It's not fair."

Fred was nodding, to the point where he should be hurting his neck. He asked again for a peach, and Estrella reminded him that he'd eaten them all. I expected a joke about him eating me instead, asking me to send forward a finger, even a forearm. But it didn't come. He was really on the nectarine kick. And gaining steam.

"I can't believe how fucked nectarines are, Estrella. They're a good fruit," Fred said, and then he said it again: "They're a good fruit. A delicious food."

"And don't forget the wood," Estrella said. "I don't think we own anything cut from the wood of a nectarine tree."

At that point, it was dark and the top tip of the sun had finally sunk into the horizon. Fred was losing the lines on the road, almost clipping a station wagon in the left lane, the next moment riding the berm and rolling on the sleep strips. If I didn't go to the bathroom soon—in a toilet, on the side of the road, or in my pants in the back of the car—I was going to pass out.

"I'm going to plant a nectarine tree when we get home," Fred said. He sounded as sure about that as he was his name was Fred. "We'll harvest the fruit for a few years, then cut it down and build something from its wood. A chair. Or maybe something bigger, like a dining room set, a table and four to six chairs."

"Or kitchen cabinets," Estrella said. "I'd like to be the only woman in our building with fresh nectarine cabinets."

I thought of the randomness of fruits, especially pertaining to wood. I knew they made things out of cherry wood—my father, before he left us, had a Murphy bed made from cherry wood, a cabinet frame the size of two of him. I couldn't think of other fruit wood, though, no pear park benches or plum rocking chairs. Nectarines weren't the only ones who were screwed—but we were talking about nectarines, and I didn't think it was a good idea to get Fred started on other fruits. I looked up and saw that Fred was perspiring even though it was cold from the air conditioning, from the sun's having been set for hours. My skin felt like a corpse, but there he was, sweating.

"I'm going to write my congressman," Fred said. After a few seconds, he laughed, and I thought we were done talking about nectarines, moving on to politics, some joke about this or that asshole from his state. But then Fred said something else about nectarines getting fucked, and I knew he wasn't close to being done.

We still hadn't crossed into Florida at midnight. I remembered a trivia question from a game show asking what was the biggest state east of the Mississippi. I thought the answer was b) Pennsylvania, but it was d) Georgia. A) New York and c) Virginia were the other choices. I wouldn't have won the money on the show, but I wasn't on the show, so it didn't really matter.

"Don't forget we have to stop for that peach syrup for your thighs," Fred said. I'm sure he was talking to me, but then again, maybe he wasn't.

Estrella then said something that made me feel better: "He's got to be starving, too, Fred. We don't want him to be skin and bones."

I was beginning to wonder when Fred's car would run out of gas, how stiff each of them had to be, how neither of them had to ever eat, drink, or urinate. Just gripe about nectarines and make allusions to eating me.

"We'll be in orange country before long," Fred said. "Oranges, they have everything. They focus their energies on juice, but they're everywhere. You use them as garnish, put slices in beer, make all kinds of shit. I wrestled in high school, and the only thing I ate my whole junior year was oranges. Not only are they low in calories, but the acid burns away at your body fat. I dropped three weight classes by Halloween."

"You should have seen Fred in his uniform," Estrella said. "It was tight and he looked like a baby in a red diaper out on those mats."

Fred was a large man now, as if he really had eaten me or someone else. But I could picture him eating only oranges for a year. He'd eaten a whole bushel of peaches that day alone, with no intention of getting any other food. No protein, no carbs, nothing. He was just wired that way, I guessed.

We saw signs for an exit two miles away with gas, lodging, and restaurants: a McDonald's, a Wendy's, a Cracker Barrel, a Waffle House, and a Krystal, the South's White Castle knockoff. I pictured myself ordering at any one of those establishments after using their facilities, a smile on my face, my $20 bill in hand. Fred's gas light was on, too, and had been for a lot of miles.

"The funny thing about Florida oranges is that they're for juice only," Fred said. "California navels are what you eat. These oranges are for juice. That's why they all say 'juice oranges' on the billboards. No one wants to get sued for passing off juice oranges as eating oranges. They'd go to jail."

"I don't think that's true," Estrella said.

"Look it up when we get home," Fred said. "If you eat a Florida orange without juicing it first, it'll taste like shit, like a glorified, round lemon. Something to do with distillation, I think."

The exit with the restaurants and gas and bathrooms was coming up in half a mile. Estrella pointed to the sign, but

Fred ignored her. I could see its lights in the distance, golden arches, golden shells, the whole lot. I pictured myself going to the bathroom and couldn't believe a half mile was so far.

"At least we'll be done with those fucking peaches. No peaches in Florida—I think it's illegal to grow them there. At least to transport them. You have to declare your fruit at the border. It's easier to transport drugs than fruit in Florida."

The illegality of peaches seemed dubious to me, but then again, I remembered I'd heard something about fruit flies destroying entire crops of this or that. Maybe it was taking oranges out of Florida, the vice versa. Maybe that's why they could only leave in juice form—to keep the flies from infesting Georgia peaches and pecans, and whatever they grow in Alabama, maybe cotton. Juicing strained the bug eggs out.

"Peaches are pathetic, really, when you think about it," Fred said. "Some king."

"What's that?" Estrella said. We passed the exit, along with a sign that said, "Next Exit 33 miles." I wouldn't be able to make it that long. Passing the last exit seemed wrong. I couldn't believe it'd really happened.

"Peaches are king here. You can find them anywhere in Georgia, buy them by the bushel. They probably fall from the trees like leaves and nobody in Georgia bothers to pick them up. Mangos are like that over in India—littering the streets and rotting but no one cares. You know, it's illegal to sell mangos because the idea is so preposterous. You can have your hands cut off for selling a mango in India."

I looked to Estrella to say something but she didn't.

"Peaches are the true king of their state, but some king—they can't even leave their own kingdom. It's like that movie about the Chinese emperor, the kid who could have everything—and I mean anything, a hundred women at once if he wanted—but he can't leave the castle. Otherwise, they'd cut off his head."

Involuntarily, I started to hit my fist against the side of the door. I asked Fred to stop his car, to pull over right away or I was going to pee in my jeans and all over his seat.

We passed another road sign that said, "Tampa 111." Either I was wrong before, or somehow, we'd gotten turned around ... then back again. Tampa couldn't be 111 miles away forever.

Fred drove on. In fact, just as I was thinking about opening the car door, barrel-rolling out, he sped up. In the dark, I couldn't get a sense of the road, how to land without breaking my neck, and so I decided to stay where I was.

"Fred," Estrella said.

We progressed onward, the car starting to shake from extending itself, the speedometer maxed out at 130. It seemed like the mile markers were visible from one to the next, Fred eating up miles one after another, like peaches. We passed a Georgia State Trooper lurking in the median and I thought I was saved, but he, for whatever reason, didn't follow us. Maybe he didn't see us. We could have been a blur.

"Fucking peaches," Fred said, and that did me in. I pissed. I was in a car, with complete strangers, sitting in their backseat, and I peed my pants. Estrella and Fred had to know it, too, because it made a sound against my jeans like a kitten stuck in a canvas sack, clawing every which way. But neither of them said anything. Nada. Estrella rolled down her window to cover the smell, pure death and only getting worse, while Fred asked for another peach, for me to check under the seat. He told me he really did love peaches then, that when it came down to it, they were good fruits, too. When I said there were no more peaches, that he'd eaten the whole bushel, he said out loud, "Fuck peaches," and drove on toward Florida, laughing and laughing at the poor excuse for a soon-to-be-dead king.

# Finding My Werewolf Mask in the Hide-a-Bed, July 4, 1994

Of course I had to wear it to the barbecue. You don't come upon something like that and not take it as an omen. Savannah's family didn't care much for me anyway, and since the feeling was mutual, acting like a jackass would be more fun than an M-80 in the potato salad. There'd be lots of kids scrambling about, cousins and nieces and nephews and shit, and if I was going to top last year's display, general drunkenness wasn't going to cut it by itself. Savannah would be pissed at me for a week or two, maybe longer, but things between us hadn't been going so hot, not since my tryst with that stylist from her shop. I looked at the werewolf mask as a sign. Wearing it to her family's shindig could do us some good, start a dialogue. Really, when I thought about how we'd been getting along, things could only get better.

I didn't wear the mask until I got to her folks'. Savannah never would have gotten in the car with me, even if she'd seen it on the back seat. Plus, I had to drive, and those things aren't really made with peripheral vision in mind. I jocked the mask, stashing it under the seat when I snuck out for a smoke, later driving off as if nothing were up. On the way, Savannah warned me about drinking too much, told me we were at the end of all our ropes, how one more incident would do us in. I didn't know which incident she was referring to, last year's Fourth adventure or the stylist with the juicy-fruit ass, but I decided either would have done the trick. I couldn't help grinning, knowing the mask was under my seat, and when Savannah asked me what was so funny, I told her about something I'd seen on the TV. With how much TV I'd been watching, that was plenty easy for her to believe.

Savannah's old man, for a rich prick lawyer, knew how to throw a bash. Some guys prided themselves on their outdoor cooking skills, wearing the apron and turning the meat with the big tongs, but not Jerry Lee Henderson. The day before, he brought in cooks, professionals who set up these steel drums they'd cut into smokers. One had chicken, one had steaks, one had ribs. If that wasn't enough to make me salivate, about a thousand ears of corn sat stewing in this giant barrel of butter. A guy he knew from the Army was setting up a fireworks display, just for us, probably bigger than what the city had planned. A band was playing oldies, and did a pretty good job with "Runaround Sue." There was a canopy. Chairs sat in rows, padded in alternating red, white, and blue. There was booze, two kegs of Heineken, one of Miller Lite. And wine—four different colors, poured by a dude in a white tuxedo jacket and black tie. When I was a kid, I was lucky to steal a brick of firecrackers from the Woolworth's. Savannah had certainly lived on the opposite side of the tracks. But for everything these people could buy, they needed some fun they couldn't put on a Gold Card. That's where I would come in.

I couldn't put the mask on right away. This was the Fourth of July, Tallahassee, Florida, and you didn't walk around with a furry rubber mask on your face. The weather on the radio said it would hit 98, but in the swamp, that meant like 120. Wolf time would wait for two things: for it to get dark and for me to put one on. I could chill out in the meantime, work on my buzz, talk with the guy in the tux jacket, sip some wines, pump some beers. Savannah would be off socializing with the women, and the men, they preferred not to fraternize with me. I'd said some things the previous year, like what I thought about NAFTA and the good Lord Jesus Christ, and from what Savannah had been telling me, most of the men, including Jerry Lee, thought she was slumming. Like, no shit.

I got away without talking to anyone for a few hours, just some *Hello, how are you*s in the food line, an *Excuse me* when I camped in front of the bathroom door. Some lady I'd never seen before asked about Savannah's and my wedding plans. Since the stylist, I don't think our plans involved a wedding, but to be honest, probably not before, either. Mixing wine with the beer might have made me paranoid, but I had the feeling everyone was giving me the evil eye, that they knew my secret, knew what would happen at nightfall. But for the most part, I was able to blend in, just another guest at the party, a friendly face in a ball cap and T-shirt, probably the guy who set up the canopy and chairs, maybe one of the neighbors, even the gardener.

As soon as the fireworks started, I tried to get out of one of the padded folding chairs, which I'd been drinking in for a while, and fell face-first into a cooler of ice. I recovered with flair, pulling myself out before anyone could lend a hand. A few people stared, but it was dark, and for all they knew, I'd stuck my head in the ice to cool off. But it was definitely time to sneak to the car.

Upon putting on the mask, I remembered how uncomfortable the damned thing was. The previous Halloween, I'd gone as the Grim Reaper, just a black cape and a dull sickle from the shed. The year before that, the werewolf. I wore a pair of jeans, a flannel shirt, and the mask. Savannah wanted to rip up a cheap wig, glue some hair to the backs of my hands, but I didn't care enough about Halloween to start attaching shit to my skin with glue. The mask was good. I was a werewolf, everybody would figure me out. It wasn't like her friends were going to look at me with my bare people hands—the mask covering my face—and wonder what the fuck I was supposed to be. Savannah called me a half-assed werewolf, but she'd called me worse, and when I told her Tinkerbell was a rotten whore, it was time to go to the party. This was our happy era, before things really started getting ugly, before we meant the things we said.

When I got back to the fireworks show, nobody noticed the mask. Not one guest, not even the kids. Everyone was looking up in the sky, watching the colored sparks against the backdrop, rockets flying above the trees and past the moon, which was only half-full. I thought about how cool it would be if it was whole, me with my mask. Over a hundred people attended the barbecue, and as I stood behind them, I started wondering how anybody gets to know a hundred people, let alone wants them at their house on a holiday. Then I realized. Most of these people were Jerry Lee's clients, tax-evaders and DUI-dodgers and other crooks. Maybe I had more in common with these people than I gave them credit for, but still, I couldn't point to one I thought I might like.

After about ten minutes and five grand worth of fireworks, I got another beer and wandered off. There was a stream running behind the Henderson property, a piss patch, really, a leak in a pipe the old man had renamed Henderson Creek. The house: Henderson Commons. The street leading in: Henderson Parkway. That was the kind of man Jerry Lee was, had to own everything, dip it in his name and let it dry, even bodies of fucking water. This had always led me to believe that Savannah and I would never last, that he'd never let it happen. Either he'd kick off or he'd see me gone, a bullet in the back of my head, someone who owed him a favor paying him in full. If either happened, I couldn't say that I'd have been all that shocked, but until then, I was going to have my fun.

Full of doe-snot and fish-shit, at least the creek was isolated. I took off my shoes and stuck my toes in the water.

It felt colder than the cooler of ice. As soon as the fireworks fizzled, my plan was to emerge from the treeline, stumble toward the kegs, maybe even put my head back and howl. People would be saying their good-byes and taking their doggie bags, and I'd give them something to think about on the drive home. They'd reconsider their plans the next year maybe. At the very least, it would scare the piss out of the kids.

As I tried to take the mask off, which took some real pulling, I heard a voice tell me to leave it on. "It's sexy," the voice said, coming from behind me. Since the mask wasn't coming off anyway, I played along. Unfamiliar, the voice was alluring, a female, and most of all, not Savannah. I turned to see who was there, who was with me, but I'd fucked up the eye hole alignment trying to peel the thing from my head. I couldn't see dick. The voice got closer to me, kept saying how she liked my teeth, asking if they were sharp enough to draw blood.

"Only one way to find out," I said, but with my nose pressed flat by the latex, I sounded like Goofy, Mickey's big talking dog pal.

I could feel the grass moving under me as the girl—her voice said she was young—approached. Before touching the mask, she walked a lap around me, asking me why I wasn't watching the fireworks with the rest of the guests.

"Canines don't like loud noises," I said. Not only did my voice sound stupid, but I was taking the whole werewolf thing way too far. If this young creature would've run screaming, left me to suffocate inside an eighteen-dollar Halloween mask, I would have deserved nothing less.

Instead, I felt pressure against the mask, something inside the mold of the mouth. It was the girl's hand, feeling the teeth. She ran one finger across the upper bridge, then moved down to the bottom. Her other hand found its way against my chest, pressed flat, worked its way down my V-neck and over my heart. She pressed her palm hard against me and moved the other hand around to the back of my neck. She pulled me to her and kissed me. She kissed the fucking werewolf mask, anybody who would give a damn staring up at the sky back at the house. I'd had my share of ladies in the past, but this kind of thing didn't happen to me very often, not anymore. Savannah would die if she found out, but with how shitty everything else had been going, I was due. Most of the time, the dog bites you, but once in a while, you bite the dog.

Things elevated from there in good speed, as the girl, and her hand, made their way south. She kissed my chest where her hand had been, underneath my shirt, rubbing at my stomach and squeezing at my ribs. Soon she fumbled with the drawstring on my running shorts. My breathing got deep, the mask choking me to death. With a good, hard pull, I was able to remove it from my head, my fingernails slashing hunks of flesh out of my neck in the process. The air, as hot and thick as it was, felt like a refrigerator. I took a deep, cool breath. Never again would I complain about going to a Henderson family party, I thought to myself, and looked down to meet my new best friend.

Crouched like a catcher behind the plate was Charlotte, Savannah's little sister, 15 the last time I checked, 16 if I was lucky, 14 just as easy. She didn't perform like someone so young, but still, I stumbled backward and pulled my shorts back up, tripping over the werewolf mask and falling on my ass.

"Charlotte, it's Cyrus, Savannah's Cyrus."

Charlotte stood up and offered me her hand, helped me to my feet. She looked different than the last time I'd seen her. Her hair was dyed black and cropped short, she had a lot of eyeliner on, and her left ear was pierced about seven times. Any way you dressed her, she was jailbait, and Cyrus didn't play that.

"I know," she said. "I thought you knew, too."

The cool air was feeling less cool and the booze swirling in my gut was making a play for my throat. Charlotte wore a flannel shirt unbuttoned to a black bra, black-and-white striped tights under a miniskirt, green combat boots up to her knees.

I hadn't seen her since Christmas Eve, and the only thing I remember was her mother bitching about the double piercing in her right ear. In hindsight, not a good strategy on Mom Henderson's part. This girl used to play volleyball and run for student council. Now she looked like MTV after midnight. Once, I'd sold her some pot, laced it with hash for the extra bite. Things had obviously elevated from there. I was one squeal away from a statutory rape case, and Jerry Lee knew every judge, DA, and crooked pig in town. Putting me away was several birds with one stone, a true gift from his God.

But selling me out did not seem to be Charlotte's intention. Instead, she declared the following: "I wouldn't say anything if I were you. Who do you think they'll believe?" She followed this with, "Sucks about Kurt Cobain, huh?" then walked away, back toward the house. Every few seconds, her form would light up with the sky, a picture flash for every explosion, making me wonder how well we'd been seen from the house, what the fireworks revealed to the rest of the party.

I stayed by the creek for another half hour, waited for most of the cars to pull away, for the real canopy-and-chair guy to come and strike the set. I dipped my toes in the drink, as planned, and sat on a willow root, sweating my dick off and needing a beer. As soon as the coast calmed, I put my shoes back on but not my socks and started up the hill. Either I'd run into Savannah, screaming at me for getting lost, or Savannah's father and a gun. Half of me wanted Jerry Lee and his coon rifle. I couldn't stand Savannah's bitching, but more than that, I was sick of the whole goddamned thing, her family, the Hide-a-Bed, my life. I'd squandered everything up to that point, missed some real opportunities, and in general, been a fuck. If my time was up, if I was going to take one in the heart, I couldn't complain. At that point, it bothered me more that I'd ripped my shirt somehow, probably on a branch, right down the middle of my back.

I walked toward the voices, the entire lawn lit by tiki torches, too sauced to determine which cluster of lights was the house, which was the stars. I heard someone say my name once, again, then a third time, before it stopped. When I got closer, I could make out Savannah next to her father, mother, and a large, male figure that could have been anybody, probably the local sheriff, maybe some client with a history of violence. Nobody was talking, but they were all facing me, watching my gait, hoping I'd trip on a divot and break my neck. I walked with deliberation, ready to face whatever they had in store. I thought about Charlotte, clenched the werewolf mask in my hand, considered pulling it on, but was afraid it'd get stuck again. I should have left it by the stream, but was glad I didn't. It was mine and I was taking it home.

Across town, where the backyards weren't called grounds and the houses didn't have names, a pathetic, crappy rocket trailed pink and white across the sky. The whole thing lasted about two seconds. I couldn't help but think that this one rocket, all two second's worth, was the highlight of some poor family's holiday, how they'd spent a week's grocery money on it, that the kids were waiting for two weeks to blow it off. Within a minute, it would hit them that life was full of disappointments like that rocket, that they'd shot their wad and it was no great shakes. Whatever had been going on in their lives, they were hoping this rocket would make it better, that all of their problems would burn away in a flash of color and a loud pop. For their sakes, I hoped they would realize how stupid they'd been, how nothing you have to wait on ever makes your life better—it just means you've spent your life wanting something else. Everyone figures out, sooner or later, that you should just blow the rocket off as soon as you get it, that you can always get another rocket, and even if you don't, you'll live. Things never really change because of a special day, of anything you've waited for, because of some pretty light up in the sky.

# Cwm

*Pronounced: [koom]*

I was showering in the men's locker room at my gym when I found out peanuts weren't nuts. Instead, they're a type of bean, a legume, like soybeans or kidney beans or black-eyed peas. It didn't sound right to me, but these two guys were talking about it and the one guy who was telling the story sounded very convincing. Nuts grow on trees, he explained, and peanuts grow in the ground, like beans. The guy he was saying this to looked as surprised as I felt. Peanuts were nuts, I'd always thought, without really thinking about it. That's why they call them *peanuts* and not *peabeans*. But the guy seemed so sure of himself, confident there in the shower, forceful and authoritative.

"Why would I make something like that up?" he said, then glanced over at me. I was staring at them, my shower long done, but I wanted to hear about the peanuts. It was fascinating because it's not something I'd ever heard before, but there it was and it seemed so true.

"I don't know," I said, thinking they were talking to me, including me in their conversation, just a bunch of guys shooting the shit in the shower at the gym, a hard workout in the books. But the men weren't looking at me or talking to me. They didn't hear me when I said I didn't know. I listened for a few more minutes, shampooing a third time, then after they'd finished and gone, I waited a few moments to turn off the water and get dressed. I wasn't in the best shape, a tire around the middle, not to mention no tan to speak of and more body hair than anyone wanted. I didn't like other men to see me, especially not the man who knew about the peanuts. This man and his friend were getting dressed in my row of lockers, but far enough down so I couldn't hear their discussion. I dressed quickly, shielding myself with my locker door until I could slip my shirt over my head, and wondered what else the guy who knew about peanuts was saying, if he knew anything else so fantastic. If he noticed I was listening.

I sat in the car in the health club parking lot and thought about the man and what he'd said about peanuts. When it got dark enough for the stars to come out, I remembered Pluto, how it was a planet my whole life until one day it wasn't. But I wasn't sure what the astronomers were thinking, how they classified planets from other celestial bodies. It was probably size, Pluto too small. Maybe too far away? I also thought about tomatoes, how they used to be a vegetable, but then someone said they were fruit, so they were fruit. Fruits grew on trees, I thought, and vegetables in the ground, like how nuts and beans are differentiated. But tomatoes grew on vines. How did vines fit in? Once, when I was in grade school, some kid raised his hand and said that W was a vowel, sometimes, like Y, but in only one really weird case, not nearly as often as Y. My teacher disagreed, told him he was wrong, and everyone laughed. W being a vowel was ridiculous. But this kid had a word where it worked. I tried to remember the word, but couldn't. It wasn't a word anyone ever used so I never thought of it again, but for some reason, I remembered W being a vowel. The man at the gym might know, and I considered asking him when I went back the next day, if he would be there, too. I was suddenly afraid I wouldn't see him again, wouldn't be able to ask him about W. I'd seen him every day I'd ever gone to the club, but it terrified me, really, that he would by coincidence stop going the day I needed him, or stop going when I went, switching to the morning or showering at a different time. I pulled out of my parking spot and almost slammed into a car passing behind me. I'd missed an accident by an inch. I had to stop thinking about vowels and beans and planets but couldn't. I wanted to talk to the man right then, about W, about peanuts, be back at the gym with him in the shower, but he'd be gone. Going back inside and showering again wouldn't do me any good.

When I got home I wanted to tell my wife about the peanuts, how they were really beans, but she wasn't there. I checked the basement, the back yard, our bedroom, but she was missing. Or just not home yet. I started dinner, a frozen boxed lasagna, which would take 80 minutes plus oven preheating. While I waited, I did the breakfast dishes, sorted the recyclables and took out the trash, and watched for my wife. I did some sit-ups on the linoleum kitchen floor, my toes jammed under the lip of the dishwasher door. Between sets, leaning against the hot stove, I stared at the package from the lasagna. I wondered what part of the food was the lasagna—the whole thing or just the big sheets of pasta. It wasn't hard to imagine the man in the shower who knew so much about beans and nuts telling his friend, getting dressed across the locker room, that lasagna wasn't pasta at all, but a type of bread. Spaghetti, manicotti, macaroni, fettuccini, all of them were round or long somehow, tubes and shafts, he'd explain, while lasagna was flat, holding other types of food in between. Bread. What I was heating up was a sandwich, a baked sandwich, with meat and cheese and tomato sauce. I pictured the man in the shower coming to dinner at my house that night, my wife using the word pasta and the man from the shower correcting her, teaching her the difference, what was right and why. He would sound as authoritative as he had at the club, not coming off as a jerk, just smarter than my wife, definitely smarter than me, wanting us to know for knowing's sake. Then he would tell her about the peanuts and whatever else he told his friend that I couldn't hear. I'd tell him about the planets, about fruits and vines. He'd already know, of course. Still, he'd act interested, a good guest, give me the credit. It wasn't something a guy like him would need.

My wife came home over an hour after the lasagna finished, much later than I'd expected. I'd waited for her to eat even though I was hungry from the gym. She made me wait longer, too, wanting to shower first, and I tried to tell her about the peanuts, how they were really beans because they grew in the ground and nuts grew on trees. My wife told me she couldn't hear me through the closed door, the water was too loud, that I should tell her when she was done showering. I went to the kitchen and cut the lasagna into three equal pieces, saving one for lunch the next day, and put out two plates. My wife got dressed, made a phone call, then sat down and told me about her day, ripping into a story about a bomb scare at her office, how she and two hundred other employees spent three hours outside in the parking lot, no coats, no cigarettes, not even car keys. The bomb was a hoax, they determined, the robots and the cops and her boss, who made them go back to work at 4:40.

"For all of twenty minutes," she said.

All night, I looked for chances to tell my wife about peanuts not being nuts, but the opportunity never arose. We watched television programs we'd always watched, and during commercials, she kept making phone calls, microwaving popcorn, running to the bathroom. She told me more about the bomb scare, how a man called, said, "Bomb," hung up, and everyone had to evacuate. It was that easy. Then we watched a movie on cable, one we'd never seen but always wanted to, with no commercials, no chance for me to say what I'd wanted. One of the actors in the movie, a guy I'd seen in a lot of things but never knew his name, looked a lot like the man in the shower, the man whose peanut story I couldn't get out of my head. Before the movie ended, my wife fell asleep in her chair, and during the credits, when I got up to brush my teeth, she went to bed without saying good night. I did some more sit-ups in the kitchen, naked, not wanting to get my pajamas sweaty, hoping my wife wouldn't wake for a glass of water or to go to the bathroom again. She didn't. I rotated sets: a dozen with my feet held still under the dishwasher, putting a dishtowel under my ass to keep it from chafing. A dozen more under the stove, then break. Under the fridge, break. Sofa, break. And so on. I went to bed when I couldn't do anymore, but made a plan: I'd go to the gym before work, at 6 a.m. when they opened, and after work, too, at my regular time. I'd hire a trainer, ensure a good workout each time—lately I'd been going to the gym without doing anything, just sauna and shower. It would be different from then on. Twice a day, every day, until I was back to my college weight, thinner, even, but filled out. Confident. Lean and a few pounds heavier than I was, muscle weighing more than fat.

# Sleeping Through Starvation

Baby monkeys, scientists discovered, are evolving much more quickly than they used to. I read this in a magazine at my proctologist's the day after my son is born. The monkeys are doing things at one month their parents did at three, and at a year, they out-think everyone in their group. By 2100, they might not only reinvent the wheel, but if their vocal cords evolve, too, they could hypothetically start going to school.

In the office, I ask my doctor what he thinks, his index and middle fingers in my ass. He laughs and says articles like that sell magazines. *One ape in a lab in Korea puts the round peg in the round hole and Boom! Mankind isn't the dominant species anymore.* He's saying this to his med students, not to me, the med students in line to diddle my prostate, the box of gloves and tub of goo next to my feet. The students laugh, taking their turns at me, and the doctor says I should eat more fiber, less pizza, otherwise I won't live long enough to see the monkeys take over.

*I just want to shit solid*, I say, and he says, *That, too.*

My wife and new son wait two wings over and one floor up. When I return, the obstetrician wants to take my boy down the hall for circumcision. Jane has made it clear this one's up to me. I had it done at birth, my parents' choice, after my older brother acquired an infection when he was nine. Under only a local, he watched them do it, a memory he says still gives him nightmares. *The surgeon, this Chinese woman, sliced into me like a steak, peeled it away like a wrapper from American cheese.* Jane just assumes I want the boy to look like me. I just don't want him to have the memory my brother has, fully sentient with a scalpel filleting his privates. I let the doctor take the boy, tell Jane it's best. I try to follow, but the doctor warns me I won't want to watch. A minute later, I hear my son scream. This, like my brother's memory, will stick with me till I'm dead.

A week later, 3 a.m., I tell Jane about the article, how baby chimps can fasten the safety pins on their own diapers, even sign to their handlers they need changed. My son has been sleeping for three hours, a new record, but Jane wants to wake him.

*He has to eat every two hours or he'll starve to death.*

I tell her this is myth, that he'll wake when he's hungry— *Who sleeps through starvation?*

*He's not a chimp,* Jane says.

I remember another part of the article, how more dad apes have been strangling their babies, what scientists suspect is a reaction to the accelerated evolution, the dads not wanting nature to pass them by. I keep this to myself as my son wakes and cries, watch as Jane sticks her breast between his lips. His screams are stifled and I know then he will live through the night, grow to be older than I ever will.

# pleurisy

bout eight years into our marriage, the dictionary started lying to my wife. A new job forced me out of town a lot more than I would have liked, so my wife, ABD since forever, decided it was her chance. She started living at the library, reading anything she could get her hands on, but it was at our apartment, with our unabridged dictionary, that the first fib occurred. **Timberwolf**, she discovered, wasn't *a large, tawny gray wolf (*Canis lupus*) found in North America and Asia; mates for life*, but instead, *a small, rubber-headed hammer used in diagnosis by percussion*. Something was amiss, she was sure, but she couldn't put her finger on it.

The night of the timberwolf incident, I was supposed to call to check in, but the battery in my cell happened to be dead. Several messages awaited me the next morning, post-recharge, and my wife didn't seem all that concerned, though she wanted to know what was going on. It was just that one little discrepancy that first time—it didn't mean anything—so I assured her she was just imagining things, that her mind was playing those late-night tricks. Her hard work would pay off for her, I assured, when I had to call her "Doctor," and she seemed to feel better about the whole situation. I told her I missed her and she dropped it.

A few weeks later, when I stepped out to pick up a few groceries, the second incident happened, this time by accident. My wife was in my office, putting away some papers I'd left out of order in the bedroom. The dictionary just fell over, she later insisted, and lay open on the floor. She didn't mean to look— afraid she'd see something she didn't want to—but the entries just jumped out at her. A **treaty**, it seemed, was now *a unit of Bantu currency*, **treadmills** were *moral obligations or duties*, and the word **treacherous** was a verb meaning *to wave or flap in an irregular manner*, which wasn't too far off, but that's not really a dictionary's function, to be not far off.

I got home from the store a little late that night, sidetracked in the parking lot by a friend from way back, and found my wife hysterical, holding the dictionary against her chest, rocking on the floor against the side of the bed, crying. She held the evidence out to me when I asked what was the matter, and even though there was no denying what she saw, I had to calm her down. I told her things weren't always what they seemed, that the mind can make you believe anything it wants. When she asked what I meant by that, I told her that *I love you, that's what I meant by that*, and *Besides, it's just a little harmless dictionary. What does it mean in the grand scheme of things?* This didn't make any sense, but my wife wanted to believe it did, because she didn't want to believe the alternative. I was able to talk her down, make her see my truth. Crisis averted.

What this all spelled out, however, was me having to get rid of this dictionary, before my wife ran across any more inconsistencies for which I couldn't account. Otherwise, the dictionary could ruin her. Could ruin us. The last thing I wanted was for my wife to get hurt; I'd never forgive myself if that happened. Before the new job put me on the road, we'd just reached the point in the marriage where we knew everything about each other we were ever going to know, settling into the routine we'd stick with until we died. I wasn't ready to give that up. I threw the dictionary in the back of my car, fully planning on ditching it somewhere as soon as the opportunity arose, as soon as the moment was right.

But the dictionary proved a bit too difficult to simply get rid of. I'd grown attached to it almost, as if it were something more than it was. I decided to hold onto it a while longer. It wasn't going to hurt anyone, not if I kept it in the back seat. After all, I'd owned other dictionaries in the past, most of them in college, when you're supposed to keep a dictionary on the desk. But none were like this one. The mystery of this particular edition, its unfamiliarity, kept my interest high. My wife, whom I really did love, served as a reliable and consistent presence, but every once in a while, I enjoyed the dilemmas and conundrums, like the fact that **reverberate** could be *a tall palm tree indigenous to colder regions*. A quick fix, once in a while, was all I needed. As long as my wife remained unthreatened, I could go on living a double life.

While I kept the dictionary hidden from my wife, other readings began leaking hints of my betrayal. The *McCall's* and *Vogues* in the bathroom started sounding like Mormon missionary pamphlets, and *The Collected Works of Shakespeare, v. II*, claimed that Ophelia had survived the fall, that she was over the prince and had settled with Ellison's Invisible Man in the South of France. Recipes for cookies called for nails instead of salt, and even the Bible lied, coming off more like a Vegas casino marquee than a moral gauge of Christian living. My wife, perplexed, asked me flat out if I'd discarded the dictionary like I'd promised. I denied everything, even though I'd been faking membership in a bowling league just to spend Wednesday nights out of the house. The lies kept compounding. I was going to have to choose between truths—the dictionary or my wife—and pretty soon, too, or else I'd lose everything that I was, the basic elements that defined me.

Before I could make a decision, a decision was made for me. The dictionary disappeared on its own, or more likely, was stolen from my back seat. There were no busted windows, no unlocked doors, just the feeling someone else was there, wanting what the dictionary had to offer more than I did. I remember the last entry I'd enjoyed, **pleurisy**, and thought that it was a good way to end—I'd never known what that word meant to begin with. Maybe *a sense of longing or distress* was the dictionary's creation, or maybe that's what the word had meant all along. Either way, it was the truth. I could have gotten another dictionary and found out. I could have searched online. But I didn't want to know. I quit my bowling league, then quit my job and found another, just to be with my wife as much as I could. She'd stuck by me, despite my bullshit, so I owed it to her.

Our relationship was different after the dictionary, but in other ways, it seemed the same. Sometimes I even fooled myself into believing that the dictionary never really happened. Most ridiculous: I thought maybe the dictionary had made our marriage stronger. In any case, my wife never brought it up again, and neither did I.

But I wonder, to this day, if she does remember, if she thinks about it, if she'll ever trust a dictionary again. Whenever she looks at me askance, or says something I don't quite follow, I feel a sort of pleurisy, think of the dictionary, and hope to one day understand what it all means.

# Fight

In the end, it was animals fighting that turned us on. S&M had run its course, swinging and swapping a step down from there; combining the two harvested few responses to our personal ad. The kids kept us from divorcing, but even their feelings were wearing thin: Neither was very good in school, or at sports.

When the squirrel snuck through the doggie door and dropped gloves with Ichiro, our three-legged Siamese, we called the babysitter and checked into the Comfort Suites by the airport. We talked a lot beforehand, too, mostly about Ichiro's comeback victory, then invoked the missionary position for the first time since the first time. We stayed two nights, turning down maid service, not even bothering to eat.

The woman at the shelter looked at us with suspicion, but the trapper from up north asked no questions. Raccoons, we soon found out, were more than a match for any dog, and opossum, despite our predictions, fought better during the day, except against foxes: Foxes had the most fight in them, that was clear. Once, when the babysitter bailed, we rented that cartoon where the mongoose battles the cobras, but felt guilty when the kids wanted to watch, too. That, we quickly agreed, held no interest whatsoever.

Like the rough stuff and the orgies, one species duking it out with another lost its luster. The combinations became less imaginative, a collie versus an Airedale, a mouse versus a shrew. Even the trapper from up north stopped returning our calls. Our last grasp pitted a gerbil against a hamster, but to tell you the truth, going in, we didn't know which was which. Expectations were at an all-time low.

What happened next, though, reignited the flame, at least for a day. Instead of tearing at each other's flesh, the gerbil initiated what would be called, by any witness, sexual assault. The hamster, a miniature Cowardly Lion, ran for the safety of the wheel, but relented, we hypothesized, just to get it over with. Later, we wondered if the hamster was female and the gerbil male, or vice versa, and what would become of this union. The possibilities were endless. We moved closer and grasped hands, squeezing tight, fighting off the rolling eyes of the kids, who, when they were old enough, would, if they were lucky, understand.

# Hapax Legomenon

*A word or form of which only one instance is recorded in a literature or an author.*
—Oxford English Dictionary

The last thing I remember before blacking out was the phantom opossum pissing on my leg. Regaining consciousness, I can see a light at the end of a tunnel and I assume that I'm dead. How this relates to the ghost opossum, I don't know, but when I inch toward the light, I find myself sliding back, deeper into the darkness. A quick diagnosis: purgatory. Four months of CCD classes taught me that souls sometimes spend centuries here. Not that I ever believed in any of that crap, but now, dead, I stare up at the light and can't help but wonder.

My agnosticism is answered when Brucie's face appears, eclipsing me to black. I've skipped centuries in purgatory and have gone straight to hell. Brucie, my ex-fiancé, is my Dante-esque punishment. I'll pay forever for breaking off the engagement, for making her—after a stint of stalking and a restraining order—take a shotgun to her jaw. I will now stare at her damaged face for all eternity.

"I found him," Brucie yells down the tunnel. Her face turns into the light and she repeats, "I found him!"

I'm guessing now that I'm not in purgatory, limbo, or even hell. I am not even dead, but in some sort of dark, metal cylinder. I make another educated guess: the iron cannon on Long John Silver 9, a decoration on a mini-golf hole.

Brucie's face reappears, her headgear scraping against the interior of the big gun. "I knew it would be me who found you," she says, and does her best to make a kissing sound, which she can't do, her real lips blown off, along with her natural teeth and a good portion of her birth chin. The ceramic prosthetics just don't cut it, and neither does the thigh skin they sewed on around her mouth. Instead of kissing, she sounds like she's hocking a loogie, which would, in reality, be much healthier for the both of us.

Brucie redisappears and another face takes her place. Too much Brut tells me it's Sanders. "We'll get you out of there, boy," he says, sounding confident and reassuring. An aluminum baseball bat, attached to Sanders' ropy, tattooed arm, soon appears down the hole. My hands are pinned at my sides, making it impossible to grab on. After explaining my predicament, the bat slides out then back in, handle-first. "Bite down on the knob," Sanders says. He pokes the 31 on the tip into my nose and eyes. I am wedged like Excalibur and my best option is to be ripped out of a cannon by my teeth.

Forty minutes, a quart of popcorn oil, and a lot of chafing later, I'm sitting next to the cannon on the soldered-together cannonball pyramid. I am in my underwear, the rest of my clothes spread over the mini-course á la a tornado. My gums are bleeding like prime rib. I feel an overbite and an underbite at the same time. Brucie sees me stroking my chin and offers up her headgear, which I decline.

"Pretty wild night," Sanders says.

"Don't remember much of it," I say.

"You never do," he says. "Not the wild ones."

I am about to say something to Sanders, ask him if Mother knows I've been found, but he interrupts: "Your mother's still looking for you."

Not understanding the situation, that Mother probably wants to dip me in the deep fryer for being gone all night,

Brucie says, "I can run up and tell her that we—that *I*—found you," two steps on her way before Sanders catches her blouse.

"Let's keep the boss unawares for right now," Sanders says. When he sees that Brucie doesn't comprehend this strategy, he explains: "A mother wouldn't want to see her boy all scraped up like Marvie here is. We'll get him fixed up then tell her a good story about where he spent his night."

Brucie stares. She is still thinking *I must run up to Marvie's mother and tell her that I found Marvie. Finding Marvie is good. Telling Marvie's mother that I found Marvie is good.* Good *is good.*

With no other choice, I move to the clincher, though Brucie's therapist has advised, via many an e-memo, against this tactic: "Do it for *me*, Brucie? It would be a big favor. You know, to *me*."

Brucie's face turns from misunderstood kiss-up to jilted-lover-still-in-love-with-ex-boyfriend-who-fears-her-with-his-every-waking-breath. "OK, Marvie. For *you*."

I instruct Brucie, who has obviously been searching for me at the Cove all night, to make her way home, to freshen up before her evening shift. Giving her the night off would be a waste of breath. Brucie's eyes say that she wants to help bathe and dress me, clean my wounds and anoint my feet, but I give her the for-*me* eyes and she's on her way.

I turn to Sanders. "Thanks. Fuck knows what would have happened if she would have found me without you here."

"Probably would have crawled down in there with you," Sanders says. He takes the last puff out of his cigarette then drops the butt down the cannon. "I can get a screen over the hole here. We wouldn't want some kid disappearing down there."

I nod in agreement, wondering what would've happened if I'd been down there headfirst.

Sanders lights another cigarette. He looks over at me, a sad state. My skin is stripped raw, one big laceration down the front of my body. "Ouch," he says, pointing with the orange cherry. Then he changes the subject: "You see it?"

"I see it every night," I say. "Pissed on my leg right before I blacked out."

"A shame," Sanders says. "Wish I could see it."

"It's not so great," I say.

"Maybe we'll see it together," Sanders says.

"Maybe."

Sanders heads toward the maintenance shed, dropping his new smoke in the cannon. He's a rock, a boulder, really, hands down the hardest-working employee at the Pirate's Cove. He shows up early, stays late, cleans the toilets, and treats every customer—not to mention me—like a long-lost child. All of this can be attributed to three factors: 1) Sanders is a very nice man; 2) Sanders is a parolee employee, on work release, and would rather mop puked-up waffle cone than go back to prison; 3) Sanders is my biological father, actually making me his long-lost child.

I'd never met Sanders before he started working at the park seven months ago. He'd skedaddled long before I was ever born, only to turn up twenty years later, a lengthy prison term for paper-hanging under his belt. He was the standard high-risk guy for the Cove, the kind we took on in exchange for having some of our building-code blemishes go unreported. Dozens of ex-cons have come to us over the years, some of whom have worked out, some of whom haven't. Sanders' appearance at Pirate's Cove was a complete coincidence.

"Guess who that new parolee is," Mother said his first day. "Prison changed him some. He combs his hair off to the side now. Used to be parted down the middle." That was my introduction to my father, who is, by the way, completely bald.

The moment Mother chose to reveal this to me, I was on my way to telling Sanders to follow the hay cart around and pick up the horse shit. Full of confused emotions, I ran out of our apartment for a confrontation, either to punch him for abandoning me or to throw my arms around him and take him to a ball game. Instead, by the time I reached him, I ended up telling him to follow the damn horses and pick up the shit.

Still, I think he knows I know. We have that kind of rapport.

I use the horse barn to get myself in order. Not only does it have a wash basin, soap, and some brushes, but it's the only building I can reach from Long John Silver that wouldn't lead me past Mother's bedroom window. Explaining where I was all night would be tough enough, but enduring her screaming and lecturing—followed by *her* trying to bathe me and dress my wounds—would push me into Brucie-like acts of self-induced violence. Instead, I choose subhuman accommodations, a choice I'd make seven days a week.

The Cove's horse, Elmer, is glue on legs. He's old, smells, eats half our profits every week, and would kick my gut out the back of my ass if I gave him an opening. Mange hangs over his head like fluorescent lighting. The only thing he's good for is pulling a dilapidated wagon for our autumn hayrides. What a horse or hayrides have to do with pirates, I don't know, but his basin and brush come in handy now.

Inside the tub, along with the grime, lies Asher, the Pirate's Cove's golf pro. Asher is passed-out drunk, the space-age rubber grip of his three wood lodged between his lips, the club head nestled between his knees. As bad as I feel and as terrible as I must look, Asher is horrendously worse off. His lemon-and-lavender striped Polo shirt and too-short white shorts are pied with mud. His over-gelled hair has shifted from debonair to ODed punk rocker. His feet are bare, yellow toenails digging scratches into the back of his own calves. And the aroma: It's a combination of tree bark and Cutty Sark. Not a pleasant combination, wet dog out on a bender.

Along with being the Cove's pro, Asher is the owner's sweetheart and a friend of mine. This is good, as the owner is Mother and Asher very well could end up my father. Asher is twenty-four, just three years older than I am, and Mother is sixty-five, going on a hundred and twenty. For Asher, there are many benefits to having Mother as a sugar momma, mainly the course pro gig, which doesn't say much for Asher as a professional golfer. The Cove has no course that doesn't begin with the prefix "mini," and our driving range is really just an abandoned stockyard and rendering plant. If you hit a ball over 125 yards, you find Interstate 65. I keep reminding Asher to take it easy, especially during rush hour, but he likes to show off, hitting balls *over* the highway and into a subdivision. Result: More work-release cons.

Finding Asher drunk and passed out is not uncommon, rather the par, though seeing him fellate his club is a first. Last night, he at least stayed sober enough to drink until he passed out. Still needing a bath, I give Asher a good shake, trying to find a sanitary place to touch him; none exist. Instead, I whisper into his ear, "Ash, I need the basin."

Asher springs awake, the club handle popping out from behind caramel-colored teeth. When I say, "Good morning," Asher grabs me by the shoulders and places the club under my chin, poking the tip into my larynx. "I don't have your money, you greasy pig. Now I'm going to snap your bird neck." The blank stare often seen in Asher's eyes has turned into red rage, one I've only seen in foiled James Bond villains.

"Ash, it's Marvie," I say. "It's Marvie!"

Asher lets go. He shakes his face loose like a dog just out of a lake and spies at me with total dilation. "Of course it's you, Marvie," he says, then brushes an invisible speck off my bare shoulder. "I wouldn't want to kill *you*, Marvie."

Asher is seven inches taller than me, and as crappy as he looked in the tub, a hand through his golden locks is all it takes to remake the big, studly jock that keeps Mother from dying, for better or for worse.

"Your mom wants to know where you were last night," Asher says.

"You've talked to Mother since last night?"

"Stumbled upstairs around three," Asher says. "She seemed worried about you, asking questions. Then she asked me to leave. I think she means for good this time, too."

Mother has asked Asher to leave before, but it's always been implied that it's until he sobers up. As soon as he's showered and reuniformed to white-bread Tiger Woods, he's welcome back upstairs, the apartment door locked for the rest of the afternoon. Mother, as iron-balled as she is, can't resist her boy-toy's tan-lined tush.

Before I can reassure him that Mother will take him back, Asher rips off his shirt, blows his nose in it, then puts it back on inside-out. "What happened to you last night, Marvie?"

"Spent the night in the cannon on LJS-9," I say.

"Go-cart guys?" Asher asks.

"Probably," I say, too tired to have thought about it before. I force myself to see pairs of bright lights, to feel ropes around my wrists. I hear morons yelling curses, challenged only by the revving of tiny, mufflerless engines. I taste diesel fumes shooting into my face. I can feel flesh peeling as I'm dragged around a blacktopped surface, rich with gravel. I feel my head bump something solid, feel myself biting my tongue—plus the opossum pissing on my leg—before blacking out.

"I'll tell them to, you know, lay off," Asher says.

"Nah," I say. I feel the back of my head and find a large lump and a deep gash. I look at my fingers and see maroon crusted blood. "Wouldn't do any good."

The go-cart guys, the guys who load kids in and out of the go-carts, have sworn themselves my enemies. They do things like drag me around and leave me to die inside cannons because of Mother's thoughts of turning Pirate's Cove into a nine-hole golf course and country club complex. Pine Crest Manor, she calls it. This would eliminate the family fun center identity and pirate theme, simultaneously allowing us to still sell a warehouse full of items stitched with a "PC" logo. Go-carts would be the first casualty, followed by most everything else. Except, of course, Asher.

Do I want this? Of course I do. I hate the Cove more than boils and sores and locusts. Working a country club would destroy the shit out of kids kicking me in the nads just to see if they can knock my pirate hat off. I want the nine-hole course and the go-cart guys know it: I made the mistake of telling them one day when they asked. It's been violent retribution ever since. To save my ass, I've offered all the go-cart idiots jobs at the new establishment. But the go-cart guys don't want to be caddies or bartenders or valets, doubling their salary with their tips alone. They want to work at a go-cart track. "Jeff Gordon started out racing go-carts," they say, and when I point out they don't *race* go-carts, they baby-sit and change a little oil, they point out how they're going to keep beating me and my big yap senseless. "Let's see you fire us if we kick the ever-living shit out of you," they yell, slapping high fives and spitting chaw juice onto the steel-toed boots they make out of Pumas and soup cans.

Asher removes himself from the basin, falling onto Elmer's hip. When Elmer brushes him off with his tail, Asher threatens to snap Elmer's bird neck. A second later, Asher is quick to point out that one of us is going to have to be first up to the apartment. "I'll go," he says. "I'm already in the doghouse." My possible future dad has a point, but I'm just as quick to point out that I am not used to bathing in front of a horse and insist on taking the hit.

"Besides," I note, "I can't manage the Cove in my underwear."

Entering Mother's apartment is like entering the hedge maze in *The Shining*. You go in, having no idea where you're headed, but if you stop or try to go back, there's your axe-wielding nutbag father. I only hope I can outsmart Mother on any given day, backtrack and get out, leave her inside to her own devices. Most days, it's not hard. Mother's sort of a maze all her own, and so as long as I'm careful, I can usually get in and out without any major gashes or slashes.

On this particular morning, my body tender, my head still pulsing, Mother's state of mind is somewhere between Uranus and the planet where the Ewoks lived in *Return of the Jedi*. For today's mood, she's chosen *Great Expectations*, the routine where she turns off all the lights, drapes dusty tarps over all the furniture, and sits in the corner of her bedroom with her old wedding dress on, pining. An open pack of Suzy Qs sits on the kitchen counter, one half of one of the cakes eaten. I'm thankful. *Great Expectations* is mucho preferable to the *Psycho* routine, or even worse, *Glass Menagerie*, where she constantly gripes on me for not bringing a chum home for my sister. I don't have a sister.

"Marvie, is that you?" Mother calls out. Mother knows it's me, as I saw her in the window watching me come in. "Marvie, bring Mother her glasses."

Even better than it being *Great Expectations*, it's a mild case: She has not referred to herself as Mrs. Haversham, and, as of yet, she has not uttered the name "Pip."

"Pip, bring an old lady her glasses and come sit with me."

Mother lost her glasses years ago, and as she hasn't left Cove grounds since I was in high school, she has no means of replacing them.

"You're wearing your glasses, Mother," I say, which she believes.

"Pip, darling, the men from the trust company came calling today. They wanted to do business, and I have to say, I don't know the right path."

I sit across the room from Mother on her decrepit ottoman. Like Asher's body, Mother's room doesn't offer many sanitary places to touch.

Mother continues: "I know how my darling Pip loves our current collocation, but the men from the trust company make the venture so enticing." Along with spewing ridiculousness, Mother is eating coconut jelly candies—imported from Finland—by the handful. They are the most disgusting pieces of food ever, but Mother can't live without them. She has a $40-a-day coconut jellied candy habit. Ballooning to over 300 pounds, it's a wonder she continues to breathe. Diabetes, at the very least, should have set in years ago.

"I've lived and worked at the Pirate's Cove all my life," I tell Mother. She enjoys it when I romanticize. Haggle, if you will. If I were to just tell her, "No, tear down the dilapidated money pit and build us a country club," she'd think it was my idea and forget it. If I just play along, within eighteen months, we could have a house on a man-made lake. A house with a garage instead of a parking lot. A *house*. I could maitre d' at a restaurant that serves cold roast duck for breakfast. I could learn how to golf. And Mother could, well, Mother could fall deeper into madness where there are no overpierced teenagers or NASCAR psychopaths allowed.

"But Pip, this new venture could allow you to marry your love, to become the gentleman I've always thought you could be."

Mother, is, of course, referring to Brucie. Brucie, who only has the top half of her head. Brucie, whom Mother rehired just because she hates me. Brucie, whom Mother thinks is my perfect mate.

"We could be happy, oh so happy in the New World," Mother says, burying her face into her bosom, looking up only to fit another coconut jelly into her mouth.

"Fine, Mother, then so be it," I say. Mother is starting to mix her movie references now, which is a sign that the real Mother—the tyrannical bitch-goddess who loathes my guts—might soon make an appearance. I continue: "So be it—build us a new Camelot, make dealings with the men from the trust company. Gone will be my youth, but I am no youth from henceforth on."

With that, Mother signs the papers.

I can't believe it—the nightmare of Pirate's Cove will be over. Officially. Mother is going to tear this deathtrap down and reward me with a better life. I will inherit something worth money. Large men won't hunt me down, and the chances of another child getting maimed or killed at our facility will decrease tenfold.

Mother conks out, the pen trailing off the page and falling to the ground. I take my bath, dousing my body with a full bottle of Bactine. I sit down at the table and eat the last Suzy Q and a half. Before long, it will be time to reopen. A day in the life of future maître d'. I can endure it. There won't be many more.

"You got a camera in your parrot, you bastard." This is the first thing I hear Benjamin scream at me as I start my evening rounds. Benjamin has been sweeping up pine needles from Blackbeard 5 for an hour, or, from his reaction, *not* sweeping up pine needles.

"I don't have a camera in my walkie-talkie, Benjamin," I yell back, then notice several park patrons have redirected their eyes to Benjamin and me yelling at each other. I cut across BB 1-4 and meet Benjamin, who is now sweeping pine needles with fervor. "I don't have a camera in my parrot, Benjamin. Look, see, it's just a walkie-talkie." I dismantle my parrot from my shoulder harness to hold it out to him.

Benjamin accepts my plastic parrot, which has a working walkie-talkie inside the beak. Benjamin presses in the eyes—the send/listen buttons—and I think he'll be satisfied when he hears the squelching of the park's frequency. An ass-manager's voice relays pleas over a jammed softball pitching machine.

"You see, Benjamin, no cameras, just a walkie-talkie."

Benjamin is afraid of cameras, cameras that can see and record him slacking off. Taped proof of him not working is grounds for dismissal, and if Benjamin is fired, he will go back to prison. Sanders has let on as to what happens to nervous freaks like old Benjy in the joint. I could see why he's so nervous.

After thorough inspection, Benjamin is still not satisfied. He turns the device upside down and attempts to open the butt. Soon, Benjamin figures out he is supposed to unscrew the feet. Two D batteries spring out of the parrot's rear and fall onto Pirate's Cove 5, one rolling into the cup. Benjamin picks up the batteries, replaces them, screws the feet back on, and hands me back my parrot.

"Sorry, boss," Benjamin says. "For sure I thought there was a camera in there, that you was planning on sending me back upriver."

"No cameras here, Benjamin," I reaffirm. I wink at him, realizing I am doing so with the eye behind my eye patch. "You're doing a fabulous job. Now I have to go see about unclogging that softball pitcher before all hell breaks loose."

"Right, boss," Benjamin says, and resumes sweeping pine needles off Blackbeard 5 with fervor.

This a typical encounter in the hellish nightmare that has been my life. Benjamin is a level-three janitor and a lazy one at that, but unbeknownst to him, he is prime to move up to a security-level position, given his violent criminal past. As soon as he is with us three months, we're giving him a flashlight and baton and will set him loose on the east parking lot. Benjamin's not having shot anyone during his string of armed robberies was a bonus, as we would've had to wait a whole six months on the baton if he had.

With the golf course papers signed, all of this is moot. Some time before winter, I'll catch Benjamin goofing off and send his lazy ass back to prison, then sit back and watch the fairways take seed. It will be a sweet life, one where violent people are behind bars, the young ladies are well balanced and rich, and drunks pay us eleven bones for two ounces of watered-down Scotch.

After getting Benjamin to relax, I head toward Davy Jones' Locker, which is our stupid name for the batting cages. A clogged softball arm awaits. Halfway there, I see Brucie coming toward me. Normally this is my time to run away, but as Brucie approaches, I notice that she has the dimpled pattern of a pitching-machine softball imbedded in her forehead. I double-take, long enough to get me stuck in confrontation.

"Marvie!" she says. "I just fixed the clog!"

I am amazed at just how deep the ball pattern is in her forehead, tire-tread deep, a-penny-up-to-Lincoln's-neck deep. It does add an aspect of realism to her cabin boy uniform—a battle scar, perhaps a cannonball from a British tall ship—that has grazed her skull.

"You did real good, Brucie," I say. "Next time, just be careful to turn off the machine before you stick your head in front of it." I say this in a friendly, sort-of kidding way, probably the nicest gesture I've made to Brucie since her mouth-blasting. Had this been some old high school chum, I would've socked him on the arm.

Of course, Brucie doesn't understand kidding. It's all criticism to her. Rejection. She begins to cry. Patrons who are watching no doubt think I've slapped or punched an already-disfigured young woman.

I take Brucie down to First Aid—which we have no fancy

pirate name for—and get her some ice for her forehead, careful not to make any misinterpretable physical contact. I tell her to kick off early, that I'm sorry about the turn-off-the-machine comment and she stops crying in at least one eye. She refuses to leave, however, as leaving would be exiting my proximity sooner than she had to. Still, her willingness to be left at First Aid alone is a good sign, a step she couldn't have made a month ago. I'm proud of Brucie, which is a step for me, a step I couldn't have made a month ago. I'm proud of myself. Pride is good.

From First Aid I redirect to the Wench's Watering Hole, the Cove's second-largest snack bar. Inside, a family of five watches Sanders construct waffle cones. Regulars. They are the corpulent bunch in matching red overalls that read "We Are FAMILY!" across the chest in white iron-on letters. The family salivates as Sanders, WWH manager, carefully lifts each waffle from its iron and wraps it around the metal shaping cone. When it's semi-hard, he fills it with frozen yogurt, which is actually just much cheaper soft-serve ice cream coming from a spout marked "Yogurt: 98% Fat Free!" At $5.95 a pop, these folks have just paid Sanders' parolee wages for the night. When the family leaves, I ask Sanders how it's going.

"Something black was coming out of the machine for a while, but I passed it off as jimmies."

This makes me happy. Sanders understands what's at stake here every night. A lesser employee would have stopped selling faux yogurt and cleaned out the machine, moldy as all hell, but Sanders knows that a happy Pirate's Cove visitor has at least one waffle cone before shipping off. He will make a good bartender at the course, someone who understands a designated driver can imbibe eight watered-down cocktails and still drive a Lexus through the subdivisions.

I amble off, wondering how we'll work it—Sanders, I mean—in the year it will take to build and grow the course. For him, no Cove, no job. No job, no parole. I predict a free club membership for some union heavy, someone who will get Sanders on his golf course-building crew and not ask any questions. I need Sanders around. Besides, he's my dad, and one day, we might actually acknowledge that.

Two hours later, the Cove nearly closed, I do a quick lap around the grounds, making sure doors are locked, registers counted, no stray skater punks hiding in the decorative treasure chests. Not ten feet from the Crow's Nest door, I am grabbed from behind and hit over the head with something heavy. I kiss the floor. Hard. Something is pulled over my face. From the putrid smell and scratchiness, I guess burlap, one of the old potato sacks patrons used for sliding down the giant yellow slide. The slide collapsed three years ago—followed by some minor-injury lawsuits—but the sacks we kept around, piled in Elmer's barn, per Mother's orders: "Just in case." I had no idea why we'd need two hundred burlap potato sacks, but the go-cart guys have found a use for one of them.

I'm positioned upright and tied spread-eagle against some sort of fence. The burlap bag is ripped from my head. Staring me down is a pitching machine. I can't make out the speed, or if I'm looking at baseballs or softballs.

"You didn't get last night's message," a voice whispers in my ear. I turn my head to see a masked man, albeit a masked man in a go-cart guy jumpsuit, the crazy leader-guy who has the Apple Jacks box logo glued onto his chest, arms, and legs.

"Must be hard of hearing," another voice says. "Maybe this will loosen his ears."

Money clinks into the coin slot

I pray that the go-cart guys only have a dollar between them. My prayer is revoked. Apple Jacks pulls out a twenty and feeds it into the bill acceptor. The go-cart guys leave, roiling off into the night. The orange "ready" light on the machine flicks on. I hear the pitching arm start its rotation. I pray for slow and softball—even tied spread-eagle, I can make slow softballs miss my groin.

A baseball whizzes out of the dark, and from the whir, I guess medium, not fast enough to kill me, but hard enough to feel. I see the projectile just before it catches me in the gut, which hurts, but is handleable. Then the pitching arm comes around again and speeds a second ball square into my solar plexus. I cannot breathe. The balls come one after another and I'm glad we are cheap and only give three pitches per dollar. Still, that's sixty-three pitches, at 60 mph, with me as bull's-eye. I can imagine nothing worse.

To put a cherry on top of the evening, the ghost opossum appears in front of me and stands on its hind legs. He looks like he wants to box and he knows he'll win. I think the next pitch will catch it in the back of the head, but the baseball sails right through the opossum's neck and into my stomach.

"Build it and they will come," the ghost opossum says. Up to this point, the opossum has never spoken to me. As if things couldn't have gotten any more bizarre. To my favor, for two or three pitches, the shock of hearing the rodent talk makes me forget my pain. But, as the opossum waddles up to my leg and pisses on me again, the next ball breaks a rib. Another baseball comes, this one slipping off the hand a bit early, catching me just below the throat. The opossum is still pissing, too, pissing more ghost piss than could fit into its ghost opossum bladder.

There are fifty-one pitches to go. I pray for another clog.

I wake the next morning, still tied to the fence, Brucie's face again in front of mine. Brucie, no longer the owner of a human mouth, is not a pretty sight. From a hundred feet, the prosthetic works really well, convinces you she has a mouth.

Any closer, it's ugly. Propped before her now, I know I must look pretty bad, bad enough to add "horrified" to the Brucie face résumé.

"I'm never going to First Aid again," Brucie says, draping her body over mine like dusty tarps on old furniture.

"Get me down, Brucie," I say. "Please."

Brucie, only 5'1", needs to climb me to get to the ropes around my wrists. Climbing me is bad. Internal bleeding that had taken a hiatus reawakens. I urinate in my pants, an army of fire ants crawling out of my urethra.

"Why would you go and do this to yourself?" Brucie asks.

I laugh, but then remember that Brucie doesn't joke. "I didn't."

Brucie keeps untying, keeps digging heels into kneecaps. Soon my right hand falls from the fence, straight to my side, slamming against the chainlink. The left follows. Brucie concentrates on my feet. As much as I don't want to admit it, she has rescued me two days in a row. I almost feel as if I owe her something.

"Brucie, it's very nice of you to untie me like this, like how you found me in the cannon."

Brucie stops untying and stands. I'm convinced she is going to take my thanks as a proposal, but instead, all she says is "You're welcome" and continues her untying.

Just when I couldn't feel worse, I do. Brucie is not only my savior, but she's acting sane. My pulverized brain starts thinking back to when I'd first met her, when I willingly dated her. It started in high school, and she was, honest to any god, not bad. Not gorgeous, but cute. She played on the badminton team and sang chorus in *Wild Oats*. Best of all, when I looked at her in the hall, she didn't laugh at me like most girls did, or look away in disgust. For the Vice-Sergeant-at-Arms of the AV Club, it was enough. I was sold.

Then Brucie started working Mondays, Wednesdays,

and Saturday afternoons at the Cove. Back in the day, Mother not only accepted ex-cons, but kids, too, from the orphanage up the river. Catholic kids, no parents, most of them criminals in training. Until some nun in a Chevette dropped her off, I never pegged Brucie for not having parents, but I envied her for it, no faceless convict dad or insane hateful mom.

Already wooed by her general lack of disgust for me, I showed Brucie the ropes. Gave her the easy jobs, too: skee ball ticket-counter in the Nest, scorecard- and pencil-giver at LJS. Tutelage led to rides to and from the orphanage, soon taking the long way, just talking. Things were going well.

Then I tried to kiss her. The first time, I went for a peck on the cheek. After, Brucie flung me against my seat and told me she loved me. I told her the same back, the only time I ever told her, or anyone, that I loved them. Brucie took this all as a sign to unzip my pirate knickers, which seemed like a good idea at the time. We were parked right outside the orphanage convent window, and I could hear the nuns watching *Wheel of Fortune*, the click-click-click of the wheel spinning. But when one of the nuns yelled out, "Larry Hagman," Brucie spooked and ran to her dorm without doing much of anything. I drove home, not bothering to redo my trousers, happier than I'd ever been.

It was all downhill from there. First came the phone calls, every day before school and work, all night after. Then Brucie started showing up at the Cove when she wasn't scheduled, pretty much whenever we were open, calling me on her parrot every three minutes. When it was time to drive her back to the orphanage, she'd get out of my car at the front gate, saying the nuns were getting suspicious and that dating wasn't allowed.

A month into our courtship, the fuzz showed up at the Cove, looking for the runaway Catholic orphan schoolgirl, a girl someone spotted sleeping on the eaves outside my window. When the cops tried to haul her in, Brucie declared she was pregnant with my child, which wasn't true, unless Brucie's ovaries were in her right palm. Still, the cops tossed me in a cell, making it known to the other inmates that I was the kiddie orphan rapist they'd been talking about on the news. I was seventeen and so was Brucie. Lucky for me, the other inmates were winos inside to sleep it off, not boy-boppers looking for an excuse.

When I got out, it was three days later (Mother's little funny), and Brucie, missing "the very fiber of my being," recanted when they wouldn't grant *her*, my accuser, a visitor's pass. A doctor's test also confirmed Brucie's purity intact. Not amused, I broke it off, telling Brucie to get bent. That evening, she stole a shotgun from Walmart, and, well, here we are.

My leg ties undone, I am forced to lean onto Brucie, to have her remove me from the batting cages to safety. Tiny Brucie, former love and current crusader, lofts me right over her shoulder and fireman-carries me toward the barn.

"Wait," I say. I wonder what time it is, where Mother is, where the go-cart guys lurk when they're not pulverizing my organs. Brucie would dress my wounds right here on the blacktop, but I'm not quite at that stage of gratitude. "The Watering Hole. Sanders will know what to do."

Brucie obeys, double-timing to our destination. Drops of blood from some random wound drip down her back and onto the ground. Brucie leaps across Cove grounds like an antelope, the drops of blood spaced farther and farther apart as we move.

Sanders, always in early, doesn't let me down. "Another wild night?" he says when we get inside the Hole. Then I puke down Brucie's back and his countenance changes. "Get him inside."

Brucie lays me flat on the Hole counter, easing my head onto her shirt, which is off and covered in my bile.

"Will he be OK?" she asks.

"Maybe," Sanders says. "I have an idea that might work

until an ambulance gets here."

"Ambulance?" Brucie says. "Oh, right." She is gone, shirtless, heading someplace that has a working phone, all the Cove's payphones removed six months ago when the skater punks kept rolling the guy who emptied them. I try to yell "thank you" in her direction, but as swift as she was with me, she is even more so without.

A sudden jolt and heave gives me a full picture of Sanders' aforementioned idea. He has placed me under the soft-serve serving spouts. Within seconds, chocolate, vanilla, and chocolate-vanilla swirl are oozing onto my skin.

"We have to keep the swelling down," Sanders says. "If only I'd been there for you. But I've never been there for you, have I, Marvie?"

It seems like this is the moment, me covered in ice cream and my own guts, that Sanders is going to confront me with Darth Vaderian news.

I can only think to encourage him. "This place is cursed for us, eh, Sanders? I mean, we've both run into some bad luck at this place."

Sanders laughs with half a heart, like someone laughs at a Sunday comic strip. But instead of saying something like *Son, you're going to be OK*, his hand on my shoulder, or *There's something I have to tell you before the ambulance gets here …*, Sanders drops this bomb onto my sticky lap: "Of course, with the whole thing being built on the rodent graveyard, our luck isn't too surprising."

With this bit of information, my parrot walkie-talkie, still attached to my shoulder and somehow undamaged, screeches with voices, angry, ballistic, go-cart-guy voices. Not eight seconds later, the fiends explode through the Hole's swinging doors and sock both me and Sanders over the head with tire irons. The last thing I see is sweet, bitter chocolate raining into my eyes, tasting a drop when it hits my lips.

To my surprise, I wake again, dodging death for a third straight blackout. The pain in my head balances the pains inside, but all I can really feel is my skin stuck to the ground, ice cream coating me like a leotard. Making matters worse, I know where I am: I lie at the feet of Walk the Plank!, the Cove's recently installed bungee jump crane.

I turn my head to see the go-cart guys, cracking their knuckles, spitting, punching their palms. "Caddies," one of them mutters, the one who favors the Raspberry Juicy Juice logos.

By this time, some of the other go-cart guys are warming up the bungee crane—it takes two or three of them to figure it out. The others throw Sanders and me to the ground and drag us to the Walk the Plank! suit-up zone. They pull our ankles up to the air and attach the leg harnesses to our shins. The harnesses are way too tight, but I take it as a good sign that we have the harnesses on. A harness I wasn't expecting.

When I think things are going to proceed from there, the go-cart leader, Apple Jacks, says, "Halt!" Up the wood-planked path marches Mother, wearing a nightgown and nothing underneath. It's the first time in over a year she's left the apartment.

"What's going on here?" Mother says. I don't believe it at first, but it almost seems as if Mother is trying to rescue us.

The go-cart guys look at each other. Apple Jacks. Juicy Juice. Curad Bandages. St. Joseph's Aspirin. A bunch of others, too—guys who don't even work at the Cove: They're recruiting from the outside. I expect the whole gang to hoist Mother up next, to send the real culprit behind the country club to her death, too.

"Hazing," Apple Jacks says, almost startling himself. When Mother doesn't seem to understand, he says, "We're making Marvie one of guys. Sanders, too."

Mother stares at Apple Jacks, deciphering what the hell

he's talking about. If mean, evil, vengeful Mother is with us today, the go-cart guys are in for the beating of their lives, Mother's hefty carriage about to whip them into the next Cup season. If it's crazy, timid Mother, we're finished.

Mother approaches. She first stands in front of Sanders, whom she grabs by the face and kisses for all he is worth, lips, tongue, everything. He lets out a quiet mumble, something about rats and raccoons and the meat-packing plant, which makes Mother laugh. The scariest part of the whole experience: Mother grabs *my* face and kisses me for all *I'm* worth, lips, tongue, all of it. When finished, she says, "Boys will be boys" and disappears back down the path, her nightgown entirely too sheer.

The way up Walk the Plank! should be the perfect time to tell Sanders I know he is my father. As we begin to rise, I look over and see he has passed out, blood dripping from where the tire iron hit his head. So much for getting the father-son thing off my chest. I peer over the edge and see the remaining go-cart guys dragging the bungee safety mat out from under our drop point. Inside the cage, our captor go-cart guys are each sawing through the cords attached to Sanders' and my harnesses. The kicker is they're using steak knives from the Wench's Watering Hole. No cop in the world would look at the clean, straight cuts and say this was an accident, actually believe that two bungee cords snapped on the same day, in the same place. But the go-cart guys have nothing to lose. They are willing to kill to keep their jobs, even if it means dying in the electric chair a little further down the line. That far ahead I'm sure they haven't thought.

When the crane stops, three hundred feet in the air, the go-cart guy decked out in Cream of Wheat apparel tells me that golf is for momma's-boy pussies. Then he pushes Sanders off the edge of the crane basket. I think I hear a bit of a pop a second or two later, but I'm not sure.

"Your daddy just lost a little weight," Cream of Wheat

says. The other go-cart guy, Snuggle Fabric Softener, adds, "Yeah, but too bad he won't be anywhere near it!"

Before I can interject anything, Snuggle sends me off. The cold alone is enough to terrify me, the whole falling-to-the-earth angle not even worth describing. I half expect to see the opossum falling next to me, biting into my shin or my balls or my eyes, but the little critter has skipped this party. As my face approaches the parking lot—I will hit approximately four feet due east of Sanders' corpse—I find only one small comfort: Brucie, my spurned ex-fiancé, is alive, and not only is she alive, she is unkillable. Not even twin shotgun barrels point-blank in the face can slow her or her love for me. She is unstoppable. I know she will not rest until she has murdered every one of my killers, even if it takes her a thousand years.

# What Haunts Me in New Hampshire

Of all the things to haunt me in my old age, it figures that I'd get the broken condom that produced my no-good kid, Gary. I've screwed over more than my fair share of women, hunted everything from prairie dogs to elephants, and even once, in Borneo, had to kill a Pakistani guy because he stole my valise. But instead of one of those more understandable specters, I'm stuck in a nursing home with a translucent prophylactic whispering in my ear. "Pull out," it says to me, and when I smack at it, my hand phasing right through, it whispers again, "Pull out," often adding, "I'm not one hundred percent intact." Two of the ribs—for her pleasure—serve as eyes, and the microscopic hole, stretching to a now-visible size, plays the mouth. As if Gary himself, my only offspring from fifty-plus years of sexual activity, isn't enough, I have to live out my dying days with the vending machine rubber that wasn't worth the quarter I spent on it. Serves me right, for all those other things I did, but at eighty-four, I wish my comeuppance had come sooner, when I wasn't dealing with this hole in my liver duct the size of a dime, a pissed-up, crooked home as my final dance hall. I may not deserve anything better, but deserving rarely has anything to do with anything.

Ezra Schermanfeld, the wheezing cabbage in the bed next to me, can't hear the ghost rubber, but if I wanted, I could unhook my IV, roll over to his bed, and fellate him for two hours and he wouldn't flinch. Ezra, like me, has succeeded in breeding, and like Gary, who lives in Alexandria, Virginia, with his fat wife and my fat grandkids, Ezra's family has never visited, his just up the road in Bangor, Maine. Both of us have pictures on our bulletin boards—Christmas cards of the whole family sitting in front of the tree—but screw us if anybody would make the trip. What I get instead are Xeroxes of the kids' report cards, poems written in crayon about Pokémon and shit, and that old condom, the lube from which, somehow not ghostly, drips on my shoulders, neck, and ears. It's enough to make me pull my own plug, to watch the line go flat as my eyes shut for good.

But I don't. What keeps me going is knowing that every first of the month I make it, Gary and his family have $2,945.38 less to spend on snack cakes, root beer, and patty melts. What started eight years ago as a sizeable inheritance is about to run dry, and Gary, his five-bedroom house, college funds, and IRAs will just have to go fuck themselves.

Since Ezra isn't much company and the nurses won't answer my call button anymore, I've taken to talking to the ghost condom, telling it my problems, even making chitchat when my TV's on the fritz. I show the condom the report cards (my family thinks straight Cs are worth a postage stamp), read it the shitty-ass poems, but most of all, I hold the pictures up, right in front of its dimple eyes, and repeat, as clearly as I can, "Go fuck with these people. They sleep eight hours a night, in soft beds I paid for. Wreak havoc." The condom always answers with a "Pull out!" but sometimes its inflection changes, and I can tell he (I assume condoms are boys) understands, even sympathizes. I can't say for sure if the condom ever haunts

Gary, but when it's not in my ear, driving me up the fucking wall, it has to go somewhere. I pray to every god I've ever heard of that it's to Alexandria. After all, Gary and the rubber met once before—albeit briefly—so maybe they could spend time catching up.

Gary's mother, the third woman of five that I had the brainfart to marry, died when Gary was just six. Lucky for me, I hadn't known him up until that point. Mildred, Gary's mom, was someone I met one night off South Beach on a cruise ship, me stowing away, hoping to get to Haiti, her accompanying her parents on a trip to Havana, just weeks before rebel forces marched in and the Reds took over. If I had any luck at all, Mildred would have been stuck in Cuba, or better yet, too infertile to carry my no-good son. As my luck would have it, they were back in the States, back in Baltimore, before the coup came off. Mildred was only seventeen at the time, and her dad—again my luck—worked for the Pentagon, doing what, I've never been told. But just before Mildred died, of MS, if I'm not mistaken, her old man was able to pull some strings and track me down. I don't know how he, or his daughter, even knew my name, but one day I'm in Chile, running guns to whomever would pay the most, when I get a telegram telling me I'd better come back to the States and be quick about it. The telegram said that a close relative was dying. Me, no longer welcome in the States, ignored the note, figuring my old man, a bigger SOB than I could ever aspire to, was finally kicking off. He might have had some money, but I knew if I set foot on American soil, I'd risk a long time in the clink, if not the noose. Dear old Dad was just going to have to die off without me at his side, and whatever money he was going to leave me was just going to have to wait.

Two weeks, a pipe wrench to the skull, and a burlap sack over the head later, I'm under house arrest at Quantico and Mildred's old man is telling me the whole story—the MS, the bastard kid, and the wedding—swearing his little girl wasn't going to die without marrying the father of her child. Seemed as though the side who paid more down in Chile was the wrong side, and those charges, along with the ones I'd racked up before, were enough to put me away for life. Blatant treason is what he called it. But—and this was a big *but*—if I did the honorable thing and married sickly poor Mildred, my record would find its way into the trash and I could raise little Gary, in the shadow of his grandparents, become the father they oh so wanted me to be.

Forty-some years later, I'm wondering if I made the right choice. For the last two, the cancer has been eating away at me, refusing to spread to anything too vital, forcing me into the most depressing, most dilapidated home Gary could find, me unconscious often enough to lose say-so. He couldn't find someplace warm, either. New Hampshire is what I've heard the locals call "the asshole of New England," which people out West call "the asshole of America." In summer, the sun comes out once every six days in New Hampshire, the food is a combination of bile and the food I shitted out two weeks ago, and ever since I got here, I've had to deal with spritely, Mongoloid nurses telling me I look just like the Old Man of the Mountain, this fucking rock formation that, when viewed from the proper angle, looks like a creepy old man's face. As pathetic as it is, New Hampshirers worship this fucking rock like some sort of Buddha, putting its image on their highway signs and state quarter. Of course, the stupid thing fell apart right after I got there, which has only made the whole thing more pathetic, everyone telling me that I'm the ghost of the Old Man, that the spirit of New Hampshire lives inside me, in this run-down, crooked nursing home. When someone tells me that, about me being the spirit of the Old Man, I say that the spirit of New Hampshire must be a bloody, smelly tumor, and everyone in their godforsaken state should just go kill themselves now because they've been aggrandizing a tumor since they stole the land from the Indians. This doesn't win me any friends in the rec room, but I've hated bingo all my life, and since I can't get it up, plugging any of the spritely nurses was never going to happen, anyway.

And then of course there's the drippy, oily condom, the broken record that keeps telling me to pull out of Mildred, to leave the frail young girl alone, to go back to the cruise ship's boiler room and hide before I get tossed to the sharks.

In this adjustable hospital bed, I'm close to the end, I know, because the drugs the doctors give me have left me completely senseless. Six months ago, some sick Alzheimer's sap stole my dentures, meaning I can't bite my tongue out, let alone eat anything but mush, so here I lie, a blob of rotting man, his fortune pissed away on tapioca pudding and thermometers up his ass, his only friend a men's room novelty that didn't fulfill the one purpose it was created for. I cough up some blood, the condom whispers, "Pull out." I stare over at the busted TV, the condom whispers, "Pull out." A nurse comes in to check on Ezra and tell me things like, "It won't be long now, you twisted piece of garbage," and the condom audibly snarls, "Pull out," then disappears, making the nurse think it was me who said it. As noted, I've been with my share of women, slept on piles of money, and have even tasted the meat of a koala bear, fresh from the bone, just to say I did. But nothing I've done has earned me this. Nothing anybody's done has, not even Hitler, but I guess Ezra, a camp survivor, might argue. If the doctors hadn't cut out his vocal chords last May.

The day I am to die, one last injustice comes upon me, as Nurse Boddington, the hound dog-looking hag with the smiley-face buttons on her ochre-colored smock, tells me I have visitors. At first I think she's fucking with me, like the times she tells me my cancer's healing, that I'm going to make a full recovery. But this time, she's pretty staid as she actually cleans my bedpan and sprays some air freshener around (even in my mouth), then empties Ezra's catheter bottle. Ezra pisses more than I blink and his piss is the worst-smelling kind, a preview of the stank his corpse will make in our room when he kicks off and no one finds him for several hours. After tidying the place up, Nurse Boddington disappears, making room for the condom to return, and when he does, he starts screaming in my ear, "Pull out!" as many times as he can. The condom's voice is so loud, I could swear Ezra actually stirs in his bed, but it might actually be my own heart giving off a beat, something I haven't heard since Boddington told me my cock and balls looked like a poodle turd resting on an Almond Joy, which was funny as hell, though tragically true.

Ten minutes later, Gary, the no-good piece of shit son who's sponging my life away, is standing in the doorway, saying, "There's your Grandpa. Say hello to him, Zach." Shifting my eyes downward, I see that Gary has not only managed to show his ugly face, but he's brought his youngest, little Zachariah. I've never laid eyes on this one before, born just after Gary stuck me up in New Hampshire hell. But his round face, stretched waistline, and open mouth convince me he belongs to Gary and his fat ewe of a wife, no doubt about it. I thought the little bastard was ugly wearing a Santa cap with a candy cane stuck in his mouth, but in the gloaming of the New Hampshire swamps, I see this kid needs to be taken out back and euthanized before he scares the rest of the patients.

Nurse Boddington is more than happy to provide chairs for Gary and the Elephant Kid—what I've always called Zach—so it looks like this is going to be an extended visit. I'd hoped, upon first seeing Gary in the doorway, that he'd dropped by simply to have me sign something, maybe even nod at some questions from a lawyer, but Gary, who is balder and fatter himself, seems to be here just to hold the door open to my casket.

"Hey, Pops," he says to me, as if he and I had had some sort of playing-catch, Boy-Scouting relationship. I think he perhaps is trying to alleviate the terror on the Elephant Kid's face, making me seem less like a monster, but a peaking of my eyebrows followed by a snarl cancels out any good gesture. After a few questions about how they've been treating me, how I feel, and what kind of food I get around here, Gary tells little Zach to go into the hallway, but just outside the door, and not to talk to anyone. Zach, as big a pussy as Gary was at that age, grabs onto his father's arm and starts to cry, but Gary, displaying some of his own father's people skills, pushes him off, and in a harsh voice, tells him to do as he's told. "Say good-bye to Papa," Gary tells him on his way out, and Zach, snorting in a tear, leaves without even looking at me.

So it's just me and Gary and the remnants of Ezra Schermanfeld left in my room, waiting for me to die, one of us hoping to have something meaningful to impart. Gary tells me the news is not good, which I know, that the doctors don't think I'll last the night. I respond by coughing up a shitload of blood, and from the tickle I feel around my abdomen, I assume a good hunk of some detached organ is now resting on my chest. Gary gets a tissue from my nightstand and wipes it up, dropping it out of my sight. This is when I wish I had the strength to confront my son, tell him I regret schtucking it to his mother, regret not going to prison instead of raising him, regret not blowing what was left of my illegal earnings on hookers and the ponies. But whatever piece of me that's wrapped up in that Kleenex seems to be the piece needed to talk.

"Tell me about my mother," Gary says. He places his hand on my shoulder and leans in close to my face, and for a second, I think the little bastard is going to kiss me. But no, he's just leaning in, waiting for me to reveal some mystical fact about his old lady. At the same time, the ghost condom—the start and end to all my troubles—appears on the other side of my head, and is singing, to the tune of Sinatra's "Come Fly With Me," "Pull out!" I wonder if Gary can hear the condom's song, but his stoic, determined face is telling me no, that he's actually waiting to hear a sweet tale of his mother and me picnicking in the fucking meadow, us telling each other "I love you," me patting her pregnant belly and her smiling like a jackass on crack.

Not wanting to rot in some military prison and become some psycho killer's fucktoy, I of course married Gary's mother, and for two-and-a-half weeks, I smoked clove cigarettes in her parents' garden while she finished dying up in her bedroom. Gary, a sissy little runt, never came within fifty yards of me if he could help it, and at the moment of his mother's expiration, refused to even look at me, the same way Zach's eyes had avoided me just moments ago. I was only forty-four at the time, but years of hard living, and two previous wives, had taken their toll. I was eleven years younger than Mildred's own father, but looked twenty years his senior. Now, after two more wives, forty years, and this pesky cancer, I must look like the worst kind of death. It's no wonder Gary doesn't visit, doesn't give a shit about me, just his sweet, innocent, dead mum.

"Pull out," the condom keeps singing.

"Brrgrrmmrrgrr," I'm able to mumble. I tried to say, "She was a tight lay," but that's not what came out.

Again, I can tell that Gary's disgusted by what he sees, but he pats me on the shoulder, and wouldn't you know it, he has the balls to kiss me on the cheek.

"Grrmmmbrrg," I say. Or, "I hope cancer's hereditary."

At this point, Gary gets up, says, "See you, Pops," and leaves. Out in the hall, I hear him tell Zach that it's time to go, and like he promised, they'd stop for some ice cream. Two minutes with his creepy, dying grandfather, and the trade-off is a cone the kid doesn't need? Just a set-up for the disappointment Zach's life will be—I'm proud of Gary for teaching the kid this lesson and hope and pray the ice cream place is closed, maybe even burning to the ground as they drive by.

With Gary gone and me only moments away from death, the condom's song stops. Or at least I can't hear it anymore. Just when I think the broken condom has abandoned me and I'll be able to die in peace, it appears on my chin and I can actually lip-read the words coming from its tear: "Pull out!" it says. "Pull out!" But the expression on the condom's face is that of genuine concern, and for the first time since the condom appeared, I get the weird feeling its message is not a haunting, not at all. *Pull out!* is a sign of disquietude. The condom isn't haunting me. It's not taunting me, either: For eight years, this condom has been trying to say it's sorry, sorry for letting me down, sorry for letting pre-Gary break through its defenses and bring such agony to my life. "Pull out!" it says again, what it's been trying to say since I tossed it out of the lifeboat and into the Atlantic Ocean all those years ago. This condom, I realize, isn't some ghost here to make me more miserable. This condom, in fact, is the only friend I've ever really had.

"Pull out!" the condom says.

"Mrrgbbrrm," I say with my dying breath, reaching out to its ghostly form. "I forgive you."

# The Death of Purple

Upon returning home from his banishment, Benedict Murgatroy discovered the death of purple, the entire color, and all its subsidiaries. Concessia had called, waking him from a fitful sleep, the receiver full of her tears, of talk of the future, of—without saying—forgiveness. Living out of a suitcase had had its effects on Benedict, none of them good. He found himself sneaking back home for clothes and paperwork, talking only to the Brooklyn-born motel clerk, even when the clerk wasn't interested in talking. He had also put on weight, started drinking beer, and watched more television in a month than he had in the past ten years. His children weren't speaking to him, not even on his fiftieth birthday, and most of his friends had, understandably, chosen the other side as well. So when Concessia's call had come, at 3:33 a.m., Ben was more than happy to throw on something from the rumpled pile in the corner of the room, to accept his wife's terms, whatever they may be. He just wanted to come home.

As soon as he'd walked in the front door, Concessia revealed the true nature of her summons, leaving Ben confused and disappointed. There was no talk of forgiveness, of redemption, of missing him, even of wanting to move in another direction. Concessia had only one message: *Purple is gone*, she said, over and over, until Ben asked her to stop. Never having heard of a color disappearing, Ben was sure Concessia was either having a horrible dream or had been drinking heavily, something she'd been doing fairly frequently, and well before any of his own shenanigans. Whatever the case, Ben was glad to be home. By morning, his body next to his wife's, it would be too late for her to change her mind. Once she was out cold, he'd be back for good. He'd make sure of it this time, no more screw-ups, no more shenanigans. If he could only get her upstairs and asleep, he was home free.

Upon reaching their bedroom, Ben immediately noticed a change. The loveseat at the far end of their room was no longer plum, but white, the whitest white he could imagine. Concessia had it reupholstered, he thought, an old couch few would ever see, a preview of what his alimony would have gone for. As Concessia fell across the bedspread, Ben went to the couch to inspect, but on his way noticed that his robe, the eggplant velour with "BSM" embroidered in white on the chest pocket, had also been stripped of color. Ben recalled what his wife had said about purple, about its disappearance from the world, and for the first time, he really considered what she'd been saying.

Still doubtful, Ben began searching for other purple and purple-toned items, anything to verify his sanity, maybe confirm Conceccia's drinking. Everything Ben thought of and searched out, however, had turned white, a stark, virgin white: the shell-shaped lavender soaps, the matching body lotion, the print of the blooming lilac tree above the toilet tank. Purple was gone—at least in their bedroom and bath—and Ben wanted to know what Concessia had done with it.

Drunk, confused, her eyes swollen from sobbing, Concessia revealed herself an unlikely suspect. She cried when Ben reminded her of the color's departure, then, upon accusation, claimed she had nothing to do with it, begged for him to believe her. Ben did. How could a woman like his wife eliminate a color from existence, even just in one room? Reupholstering was one thing, and bleaching, several times over, might explain his robe. But the identical little soaps? The lotion? A print he'd bought her 30 years ago? In his extended-stay motel, he'd noticed no such absence, everything beige and brown, while the road home held no evidence either, all blacks, yellows, reds, and greens. Ben couldn't be sure if purple's disappearance coincided with being home again or not. But it didn't matter, as he was indeed home.

More of a question than how Concessia could have done this was why. Revenge? Of all the ways Concessia could get back at him, why purple? Purple was innocent of all wrongdoing, unrelated to himself in every way. Ben favored green. Purple wasn't even a symbol of anything he could think of, nothing to do with him. Royalty? A dubious connection. Christ? Ben was agnostic. Attacking purple just didn't make sense.

Convinced Concessia was innocent, Ben traveled to his den to turn on the television, to see if the epidemic was widespread. At first, Ben had no way of telling—nothing on any of the channels he searched displayed any purple—but at the same time, they didn't *not* display purple. It wasn't until Ben's surfing fell on a grocery store commercial, a sale at the local chain, that his fears were confirmed: Coke products were fine, as were hot dogs and Saran Wrap. Produce, however, gave Ben his answer. While strawberries appeared red and unaltered, grapes—purple grapes— appeared white, not the yellow of white grapes, but the same white he found up in his room, the whitest white he'd every seen. Purple had vanished, it seemed, from his house, the grocer's, and from where else, he could only guess. Concessia couldn't have done this. There were greater forces at work here. Ben began to feel the same terror as his sweet, forgiving wife, and he felt awful for suspecting her, of making her feel responsible, untrustworthy.

Reports of purple's demise soon clustered every channel. Grayed, respected reporters told tales of the epidemic, of how definitively the color had been removed, of the pandemonium and chaos that ensued, riots on every continent, crowds demanding answers from clueless leaders. One report called the incident "... the death of an old friend," as if a former president or an old actor had finally succumbed to the ages. Whether purple would ever return was the question on most lips, but no answers seemed imminent. For reasons Ben did not understand, his town sounded its air raid siren, huddling its masses into their basements, into shelters, causing an unnecessary local stir. Everyone was lamenting the extinction of purple. No more mauve. No more orchid. No amethyst or violet. Anything that contained a hint of the color changed to white. A purification, Ben thought, but of what?

As Ben watched the newscasts, Concessia, collected, joined him, watching the reports just as intently as he did, the first time Ben had ever seen her take interest in the news. Video feeds of scientists checkered the screen, talking heads presenting their theories, the occasional splash of blinding white accessorizing the square they occupied, be it a tie, eye shadow, or veins pulsing from their necks. All had theories. One expert pointed to the polar ice caps melting, another to the ozone's depletion, while another cited a long-after effect of nuclear winter, Three-Mile Island, Chernobyl, or perhaps one kept secret, a recent incident—very, very recent. A fourth theorist, a controversial theologian, pointed his finger at a terrorist attack, our enemies striking again, this "unholy sabotage" a million times more creative and a million times more demoralizing than anything they'd pulled off before. Every channel hosted its own panel, none of which agreed with any other, not completely, other than the fact purple was indeed missing.

By day's end, vigils for purple had sprouted across the country, the world, nations with every creed, color, and belief. Ben and Concessia, sitting arm-in-arm on the leather sofa, enjoyed the practical demonstrations the most, buckets of blue paint dropped into buckets of red, and like magic, their dark contents mixing to white. The trick became old, however, as did close-ups of the color wheel. By the nightly news, purple's expiration fell from the headlines, at best the first story after the first break.

Ben and Concessia had had their fill by that time, a whole day and night later, purple's demise no longer holding their interest, just another fact, a day in history they would never forget. It would grow to have nostalgic bearing more than anything, like the yearning for an old song or a restaurant they'd once enjoyed but could never find again. Their children all called, which they found odd, especially when none of them were surprised when Ben answered, or spoke to him in a curt manner. But they did not stay on the line long, citing other calls to make, other people to attend to. Friends phoned, too, one whom they hadn't spoken with in years, the best man at their wedding, living on the coast now, his wife dead from cancer, him not far off himself. Then the house was quiet, save the tolling, every fifteen minutes, of an old clock on Ben's desk, a sound he'd missed while he'd been away.

In truth, purple being gone didn't change their life much at all. Purple, like their youth, became a memory—a good one—but like any memory, firmly set in the past. They'd talk about purple again, if it came up, and sometimes they'd specifically wish they could see it, just one more time, before they died. If they would ever have grandchildren, they would tell stories of purple, of how amazing it could be, fib how it was their favorite color, how unlucky the children were to live in such a time that boasted nothing like it, nothing nearly as grand. They'd try to describe it and the children would pretend to understand, nod, then look away. But otherwise, purple would be gone. Purple was extinct.

As Ben and Concessia marched up the stairs for bed that night, they thought nothing more of purple, of its sudden disappearance, of anything that had happened that day. Instead, they slept in each other's arms, a new day ahead, as full and complete and normal a day as they'd ever had or would have in their entire lives.

# Acknowledgments

The author would to thank the following people, without whom this book would not have been possible: his parents, Leonard and Dolores; his siblings, particularly his sister Nancy, who painted the cover; the rest of his family; his teachers: Michael Kulycky, Nancy Roberts, Mike Madonick, Richard Messer, Fred Zackel, Wendell Mayo, and especially George Looney and Jean Thompson; his students; Lawrence Coates, Erik Esckilsen, Seth Fried, Rick Jones, Paula Lambert, Donna Nelson-Beene, Tom Nondorf, Aimee Nezhukumatathil, Dustin Parsons, Larissa Szporluk, and Gabriel Welsch; the folks at Dzanc: Steve Gillis, Dan Wickett, and Steven Seighman; all the editors who took the stories; his friends; his coworkers; and most of all, Karen and Ernie, who give him reason for everything.